King of the Streets, Queen of His Heart 2

A Legendary Love Story

Porscha Sterling

Text **PORSCHA** to **25827** to keep up with Porscha's Latest Releases!

To find out more about her, visit

www.porschasterling.com

Published by Leo Sullivan Presents

www.leolsullivan.com

Contains explicit language & adult themes suitable for ages 16+

They endure...

Chapter One

SHANECIA

I awoke in a daze but totally conscious of the fact that I was in trouble. The kind of trouble that could end my life just while I was at the point where I thought things were finally going my way.

I was a student, fighting my way towards a degree that many people believed didn't belong to kids like me who were the project of the ghetto. Setting aside the issues of my mother being addicted to dope, my life was going just as I wanted it. I'd even found love; not the kind of love that I'd imagined for myself, but it was still the kind that seemed pure and right to me.

Legend was everything that I didn't even know I wanted and, although I was unsure about his lifestyle, I was ready to deal with that as long as I was by his side. Unfortunately, the consequences of his dangerous life were affecting me faster than I'd been prepared for and now I was tied up in the back seat of his enemy's car.

"Aye, she's awake," a voice said to my side, making me pull my attention, for the first time, to a man who was sitting in the back seat across from me.

The voice sounded familiar so I turned to where it came from and squinted. Trying to steady my eyes, I wanted to focus on his face but I couldn't because everything around me was dark. I continued to struggle to see until I finally realized that I was blindfolded. I couldn't see shit.

My head felt like it had been pumped full of helium and was floating above the clouds, totally detached from my body. I was high. I had no idea what had been in that syringe that Mello stuck into me, but whatever it was had me feeling a sense of euphoric paranoia that I'd never experienced before.

"Already? Fuck…that shit in the syringe should have knocked her ass out for at least an hour!" Mello fumed from the front seat.

Something about his response tickled me and I began to laugh. I felt the man next to me shift in his seat and I knew his attention was on me. Just the thought of the bewildered look that probably was on his face made me laugh even more until I was overcome by loud, hysterical guffaws that totally shook my body and eventually were accompanied by a fit of hiccups.

The force of my head rubbing against the seat lifted the blindfold some at the bottom so I could see a tiny sliver of light. My eyes focused a little but not enough to see. My vision was too blurry to make out anything except the faint outline of solid objects around me.

"Why can't we kill her already?" the voice to my side said, oozing with disgust as he peered at me. "Dead or not, we can still get that fuck nigga to come looking for her. You know his sucker for love ass will try to save his bitch whether he knows she's alive or not."

I laughed harder until I could barely breathe. My arms were tied and pulled behind my back so the more that I laughed, the harder they were being tugged at the socket which brought on so much pain that I wanted to cry out in pain but I couldn't. My body was doing its own thing, totally independent of my mind. Tears slid down my cheeks as I laughed on.

"Sucker for love or not, that nigga ain't stupid and he gone wanna hear from his bitch before he moves. He not gone walk into a trap unless he knows her ass is alive. Once he hears her speak, we can bust a cap in her crazy ass and then he'll be next. And then I'll finally be done with this cocky muthafucka," Mello replied in a calm, mellow tone that I figured was the reason behind his name.

My laughter began to die down and I was grateful for it because the aching in my stomach was becoming almost too much to bear. My head bobbed back and forth as Mellow continued to drive, and I started to see spots in front of my eyes while my heart raced in my chest. I blinked in rapid repetition, wondering whether or not I was diving between various states of consciousness. From somewhere deep in the back of my mind, I felt like I heard a phone ring. Shaking my head, I tried to jar myself awake. I shook my head over and over and over again.

"Bitch, what the fuck are you doin'?" the voice next to me inquired angrily. The next second, I felt cool steel placed against my head. I wasn't too out of it to not know what that was.

"Nigga, shut the fuck up! I'm tryin' to use the fuckin' phone!" Mello shot back before answering the caller. "What you want? I'm in the middle of—"

So I did hear a phone! I thought to myself.

Somehow the thought of myself trying to shake myself awake when I actually was awake, sent me into another fit of laughter as Mello tried his hardest to speak above my giggles.

"WHAT THE FUCK YOU MEAN SOMEBODY SHOT UP MY SHIT?!" Mello roared, the sound of his thunderous voice making my ears ring.

"Aw shit!" the man next to me cursed.

His attention diverted from me for the moment, he pulled his banger away and I mentally exhaled my relief.

"FUCK!" Mello shouted after ending the call. "Them niggas shot up my fuckin' house. I gotta get over there now. They say five-0 all over my shit right now."

"Uh...we can't go over there *now*. Not with this bitch tied up back here!"

The pause that followed let me know that Mello had totally forgotten about my presence in his anger towards his new situation.

The tires screeched and my body catapulted right as he made a sharp turn. My head hit the side of the door making the black spots in front of my face turn into stars and stripes.

"We 'bout three minutes from the meet up spot. I'mma drop her ass off at the restaurant where the other niggas at and you can fill them in on what's good while I go get them pigs out my shit," Mello decided.

We drove on in silence as my mind raced between lucid thoughts and the random ramblings brought on by my current state due to the drugs in my system. I couldn't focus enough to be afraid or to plan my escape, but one thing that I did know was that if something didn't happen soon, I would die.

"Get ready to grab her ass and get out," Mello grumbled as the car started to come to a stop.

The man next to me didn't readily respond but I felt his hand on my legs as he grabbed roughly at the ropes holding me in place, tightening them with each tug.

Agonized from the pain of the ropes digging into my flesh, I grunted when he pulled me towards him with one hand gripping the knot around my neck and his other hand on the door handle. Blinking down hard, I tried once more to focus my vision but I couldn't see a thing. It was like looking through beer goggles. Even if I wanted to, there was nothing I could do to save myself.

Suddenly, a loud smashing noise that could only be made from metal clashing against metal erupted in the air, as my body was jarred forward from the force of the powerful blow of something behind us. Unable to brace myself, I slammed against the back of the front seats but my back hit the cup holder in the middle, sending a shock of sharp pain through my spine.

"What da fuck?!" Mello roared.

Before I could fully get myself together, Mello slammed his foot against the gas and I catapulted backwards as he accelerated.

"Fuck! Them niggas behind us," Mello grumbled as I felt him bob and weave through traffic at high speed.

I bit my bottom lip, feeling a wave of nervous laughter building up inside of me. I was still feeling the effects of the high but I could also feel my body growing weak and my head was still spinning.

"SHIT! Th—they can't catch up to us, Mello! FUCK!" The man

next to me began moving around in his seat as he twisted around to duck down in the seat.

Blinking long, I tried to clear up my vision so I could look at him but before I could focus on him, he cracked me over the head with the butt of his gun, sending my head reeling backwards on the seat.

"Fuck, they are right on us!" Mello said, seemingly more to himself than anyone else.

"How the fuck he find us?! They know you got this bitch?"

"Hell yeah. I sent him a picture of her ass right when we tied her up and told him to hit me up if he wanted his bitch back," Mello responded in a way that also warned the man he was speaking to that he'd better not question his judgment on that.

"He ain't gone stop until he get her. We gotta toss this bitch out or else we both dead!" the man next to me spoke with a trembling voice. He was terrified and as high as I was, I could still pick up on it.

"SHIT! FUCK!" Mello cursed as he hit the steering wheel with so much force that the horn honked and the car swerved in the road.

"Naw, keep her back there and hold her tight. I can lose these niggas!" Mello said in a calm tone, his voice returning back to normal.

"Okay, but—"

Craaaaaack!

Rat-a-tat-a-tat-a-tat-at-tat-ata-tat!

Eeeerrrrck! Screeeeeech!

My body slammed right as Mello took a sharp turn and slammed harder on the gas, making the car jump forward as bullets came crashing in through the back window.

"Push her ass out the fuckin' door!" he ordered from the front seat as he continued to drive and dart through traffic. "I'mma pull the fuck over and you swipe her ass out the fuckin' car!"

"You gotta slow down so I can get the door open!"

"Nigga, you want me to slow down to let that bitch out or you want to catch a hot one to the dome? Them niggas shootin'! Either you bring your head up and bust back or push her ass out the fuckin' car!" Mello ordered and I felt my heart begin to race.

We were in the middle of a high-speed chase. Even in my current state, I knew that if they pushed my ass out of the car, there was no way I would be able to survive the fall. A sense of relief passed over me when I felt the car begin to slow down before jerking to a halt. The man next to me moved quickly, opening the door beside me before shoving me right out the car onto what felt like wet grass and mud.

Screeeeeeeeeccccccch!

A rush of wind blew against my cheek as Mello took off, leaving me confused and disoriented. Black spots erupted once again in front of my eyes and I felt my heartbeat began to speed up in my chest, to a tempo so fast that my mind couldn't keep up with it. Struggling to breathe, my mouth fell open as I gasped like a fish, urging my lungs to take in the air that it so desperately needed. The siren going off in my head grew louder, making the pain in my skull nearly unbearable. I felt tears running down my cheeks as a cold feeling fell upon me. The quickened sound of footsteps approaching, slogging through the wet mud, heightened the pain in my head. My mouth was agape but only silence took the place of my agonizing plea for mercy.

"Neesy?" I heard Legend call out to me.

"Legend?" I was able to squeeze out between my dry lips.

I felt his hands on my face but they were cool against my burning skin.

"Neesy, are you hurt? What's wrong?"

Before I could answer him, the siren in my head became a blaring horn. A sparkle of colors erupted before my eyes, and I blacked out.

Chapter Two

SHANECIA

Beep! Beep! Beep!

The intermittent droning of a machine tugged me out of the most unsatisfying sleep I'd ever experienced. My head felt like it was pulsating along with the beat. Groaning, I tried to pull open my eyes but they felt unnaturally heavy.

What happened to me? I thought as I contemplated going back to sleep to stop the dull, painful throbbing of my head.

But then the memories slammed into my mind like a Mack truck and my eyes snapped open as I took in a sharp breath. The last thing I remembered was being tossed out of a car and hearing Legend's voice. Where was I?

When I opened my eyes, they landed on Maliah, who was sitting by my side with her mouth partially open and her eyes wide as if unbelieving that I was awake. I blinked a few times and then frowned at her.

"Damn, you gone speak or just stare at me?" I mumbled, slurring my words while shifting in the hospital bed. It felt like cardboard on my back but, for some reason, I couldn't move too much. I suddenly became aware of the I.V. in my wrist and the oxygen tube blowing frigid air up my dry and crusty nose.

"Neesy! I'm so glad you're awake," Maliah whispered as she stood up and ran over to me. She had tears in her eyes.

"I've been so scared, I—"

"Scared?" I asked, then I took a good look at her. Her face was puffy, her hair was a mess and it looked like she hadn't slept in days.

"How long have you been here? Hell…how long have *I* been here?"

"You've been out for two days," Maliah told me with a grim tone. Then she opened her mouth and her bottom lip began to tremble. She started to say something but then changed her mind suddenly and looked away.

"What is it? What is it that you aren't telling me?" I asked, snatching the oxygen tube from my nose. Then a thought came to me.

"Danny! Oh God, so you know about Danny…"

Shaking her head, Maliah frowned and rubbed her eyes.

"Danny? Neesy…I already know he's de—No, it's Tan. She…"

Maliah bit her lip before moving closer to me and grabbing my hand. Tears began to fall down her smooth, golden cheeks and I felt my heart rate start to speed up in my chest. An icy feeling slid down my spine as I waited for her to speak, my mind already churning with possible endings to her sentence.

"She's been shot, Neesy!" Maliah finally spat out as she began to cry more heavily. "I've been hoping you would wake up because I can't take this shit right now. Both of you at one time…I just can't—"

"Shot?!" I repeated, snatching my hand away from Maliah. "She got shot? How…where is she?"

Please God don't tell me my sister is dead. Don't tell me she's dead. Please GOD…DON'T!

"Sh—she's in ICU but it's not good, Neesy. Darin's been with her but the doctors are saying there is nothing more they can do... she has to just wake up on her own. This shit is fucking me up because…I couldn't stand Tan but she's my cousin. I love her! And then you…"

"I have to go see her," I said. I reached down at grabbed at the I.V. in my arm. Biting my lip, I removed the tape and snatched it out.

The machine that was beeping was connected to my chest by sticky pads. I pulled them off and the beeping became a blaring long tone. Before I could reach out to shut it off, the door burst open and three nurses barged into the room with panicked looks on their face.

"I'm fine!" I told them with one hand to my pounding head. "Please…just turn this off!"

"Ms. Jones, I'm happy to see you're finally awake," a young brunette nurse said with a pressed smile, as she walked over and pushed a button to stop the machine's wailing. She signaled to the other two that they weren't needed and then turned to me.

"How are you feeling?" she asked as she quietly assessed my condition with her eyes. She positioned her body as if she were about to block me from going anywhere but just from looking at her, I could see she only weighed about 120 pounds. She couldn't stop me if she tried her hardest.

"I'm fine," I replied curtly. "I need to go see my sister in ICU, so please excuse me."

"Ms. Jones, I need to speak to you and check a few things to make sure you're okay. You had a lot of drugs in your system when you came in here and—"

"I'm fine!" I repeated much louder although I felt myself getting woozy. "I need to see my sister and then I'll be leaving out of here. Thank you."

And with that, I stood up from the bed, sidestepped the nurse and pulled my flimsy gown tight around my body. Looking at Maliah, I waited for her to get up and lead the way. With her slanted eyes pointed down at the ends from grief, she stood up and walked towards the door. I was right on her heels, trying my best to stay calm, but my mind was reeling with thoughts as I wondered what in the world had happened to my sister.

Never in my life had I seen Darin so distraught, beat up and distressed in my life. He was always the one who kept us positive, despite our circumstances, but as I stared at him sitting by Tanecia's side, it made my heart cringe with emotion. He was torn up inside and it was all over his face.

Slowly, I walked up to her bedside. It wasn't until I was standing right next to where he sat, looking down at Tanecia, that Darin finally noticed my presence in the room.

"Neesy, you're awake," Darin said, giving me a small smile that didn't reach his eyes. "They said you would come to soon."

I nodded my reply but my eyes were on Tanecia. She looked so pale and lifeless. It was like she was already gone. She was a shell of herself. Her spirit seemed to have left her already. There was a droning sound coming from the machines in her room. It was obvious from the way that her chest rose and fell in a rhythmic, unnatural manner that one of them was controlling her breathing.

Tears clouded my sight and I was grateful for that. I didn't want to see my sister like this.

"Who did this?" I asked, turning to Darin.

From the way he clenched his jaw in anger, I already knew the answer to my question.

"They found her at Mello's spot. She was shot twice and left for dead," he said through his teeth.

"What was she doing there?" I asked him. "Did he take her?"

Sighing, Darin ran a hand over his face and shook his head. "No. She told me she was going somewhere a few weeks ago. I had a feeling she was still fucking around with that nigga because she was acting strange. When I got here, I looked through her phone while she was in surgery and she's been texting him and shit. They were still fucking around."

Shaking my head, I looked back at Tanecia before tearing my eyes away.

"Mello did this…he must have found out about Legend. That

she gave Legend information on him. He—when he grabbed me, he was in mama's house and he knew that I was with Legend. He planned on using me to get to Legend and then killing me," I thought aloud.

"See, this is the type of fuck shit I was talking about!" Darin said angrily. He stood up and I became suddenly aware of how much he towered over me.

"Y'all fuckin' with these street niggas and you think it's a game. Well, it's all fun and muthafuckin' games until somebody get fucked up for real, huh? You walkin' around here with stars in your eyes thinkin' it's all cool and shit bein' a school girl and datin' a gangster. This shit ain't a game! It's very real!"

Salty tears fell down my cheeks. His words stung because he was right. Both Tanecia and I had almost lost our lives in the same day, and it was because of the men we chose to mess with.

"Darin, it's not her fault," Maliah started. She walked up behind me and draped her arm around my shoulders.

"You can't blame Neesy for what happened to Tanecia and vice versa. Both of them are grown and they made their own decisions," she told him.

Cutting his eyes at her, he gave her a look as if he wanted to ask her to leave.

"Why are you even in here, Li-Li? You don't even like Tan," he asked rudely. I felt Maliah stir nervously beside me once she was reminded of the truth.

"I think both of y'all really need to leave," Darin continued. "If she has any chance of waking up, she'll need positivity around her and it can't come with the three of us in here together."

Cutting my eyes at Darin, I contemplated reminding him that I was Tanecia's sister and the only one truly allowed to be in her room in the first place. But instead, I held my tongue, took one last look at Tanecia and then nodded my head. I didn't want to see her like that any longer...I couldn't stand it. She looked like she was already dead. But someone had to stay with her and if Darin wanted to, I would allow him to for now.

"Li-Li, let's go," I said with a sigh. "Darin, please let us know if anything changes. I'll be back up here to check on her."

He made a grunting noise instead of responding and I felt a twinge in my chest. How he was acting was hurting me but I tried to remember that he was hurt himself. At the end of the day, Tanecia had been under his care, and he'd failed to protect her. That had to be fucking with him. The same way me being in the hospital should have been fucking with Legend.

"Where is Legend?" I asked Maliah as soon as we walked out of Tanecia's room.

Feeling like someone was watching me, I looked over my shoulder. There was a man standing a few paces down looking right at us. He was dressed in all-black street clothes and was tall, with a muscular build and long dreads braided down his back. He had tattoos on his face, all small, but I couldn't ignore the teardrops next to his eyes. The hair on my arm rose up at attention.

"Li-Li, I think we're being watched," I whispered under my breath, trying not to cause attention to myself by seeming too alarmed.

Maliah looked over her shoulder. "Girl, that's just Brandon. Some beefy dude from Legend's team that he ordered to watch over you."

"Oh," I said, feeling some kind of way that Legend hadn't stayed to watch over me himself. Maliah seemed to sense my feelings.

"He left me his number to call him if anything happened, but I haven't seen him since they brought you in and stabilized you. They told us to give you some time to rest and you should wake up. After he heard that, he left," she informed me.

Hearing that Legend hadn't bothered to visit me since I was brought to the hospital, messed with my head a little. Especially after seeing Darin refuse to leave Tanecia's bedside. I tried to brush it away, but I know the disappointment I felt showed through all over my face.

As we approached my room, a thought occurred to me and my stomach flip-flopped as I thought about the words I needed to say.

"Li-Li, I gotta tell you something," I said as soon as we walked into my room. The nurse was gone so the room was completely empty and I was grateful for it.

"What is it?" she asked, her eyebrows knitted tightly together, creating small worry lines on her honey-brown face.

"That day…right before Mello took me, I got a call. It—it was from Danny. I know you don't believe me but I swear it's true! He said he was alive and—"

"Neesy, stop fucking with me!" Maliah gasped, placing her hand over her chest. "Danny?!"

"Li-Li, I swear…I know I had drugs and shit in my system but I swear to God that I wasn't imagining that shit. It happened *before* Mello injected me. He called me…he said he's been calling you but you won't answer," I informed her.

Running her hand through her hair, fresh tears came to her eyes and she sat down in the chair next to her. Her pupils moved back and forth rapidly as she thought about my words. Then, she reached into her pocket and grabbed her cellphone and began scrolling.

"This number has been calling me but the caller ID said 'unknown number'…I haven't been answering it. Neesy, *are you sure?*" she asked me once more with her eyes squinted.

"I'm positive. He said he was alive…had got out of surgery and he was trying to reach you. He said he was at Jackson Memorial."

Without even asking, I could tell by the look on Maliah's face that she was torn between whether she should leave my ass and speed over to Jackson Memorial, or make sure I was taken care of first.

"You can do whatever you need to. I'm going to call Legend to come pick me up because I don't want to stay here. I can get better at home," I told her.

Seeing the look of relief that immediately passed over her face stirred something inside of me, and I felt unsettled that she was so eager to go check on Danny.

"Li-Li, just be careful. I know that you've been dealing with Murk and even though he claims y'all ain't official—"

"Neesy, be for real! I'm not stupid…I can't let myself go back to

Danny no matter what, regardless of what Murk and I have going on. I just want to know that he's alright and move on. You know, he doesn't have anybody and…"

Her voice trailed off once she realized she was diving right back into the same trap she always laid for herself when it came to Danny. He didn't have anyone else but her, and that fact always made her feel responsible for him. It was a weight that she needed to let go.

"He's my babies' father and I just want to make sure he's okay. As soon as I can verify that he's well, I'm out."

I nodded my head but I didn't believe her for one second. Danny was Maliah's weakness and he'd always been that. Her babies were her excuse for dealing with him. She was treading on dangerous ground but I didn't even have the energy to press her on the issue. Besides all that, I knew she wouldn't listen. A woman hopelessly in love with a worthless man never did.

"Just be careful. I can't tell you what to do, but listen to me. Murk is a loose cannon and, even though he has a hard time voicing his feelings, anybody with eyes can see he cares for your ass. Don't be stupid."

Maliah's cheeks flushed red and she gave me a look that told me she was offended by the obvious doubt in my voice.

"I know what you're thinking. But give me some credit. Every woman has been stupid over a man a few times in her life, but I'm past that when it comes to Danny. Trust."

Biting back the opportunity to let her know that I've never thought of myself as stupid over a man, I let it go and simply nodded my head. I was beginning to feel dizzy and I didn't have the patience to be going back and forth with her.

"I understand."

I reached out and walked towards her to give her a hug and kiss her cheek. "Go ahead and see that he's doing okay but promise me that you'll hit me up later, okay?"

"I will," she said with a sigh.

Sitting on the bed, I grabbed my phone off the table next to me and waited until she walked out the door before turning it on to text

Legend. It was nearly dead, but I had just enough battery left to send him a quick text to let him know I was up and I needed him to come take me home.

When he didn't respond right away, I leaned back on the soft, fluffy pillows and closed my eyes. The few moments that I'd been awake had brought on more pressure than I'd expected. Sleep was beginning to be more preferable to being awake and dealing with my new reality.

Chapter Three

LEGEND

I looked from Quan's face, to Dame's and then finally to Murk's. Each of them had different expressions because they all had different shit on their mind. The last few days had shaken our focus a little, but we were dealing with all the bullshit the best way we knew how: by terrorizing some unlucky ass niggas.

"Let's move."

Without another word, we all jumped out of my ride and walked towards the apartment across the street from us, holding our bangers at our side. The block was live…it was the middle of the day and everyone was outside bearing witness to our impending crime but we didn't give a shit.

From my peripheral, I could see mothers running out into the street, scooping up their babies, and other people running into their homes. A few curious niggas simply stood up and watched, knowing damn well that seeing all four D-Boys together packing some major heat meant some major shit was about to go down.

"Murk," I called out but he was already a few steps ahead of me. He shot the doorknob of the door and kicked that bitch open so hard that the security chain on the door was snatched straight out, giving us open access.

Quan and Dame stood watch outside in case anybody decided to get bold, and Murk and I ran inside with our guns pointed straight ahead.

"FUCK NIGGA, I KNOW YO' ASS IN THIS BITCH!" I yelled out, firing off a few shots as we stormed into the house. "Get your bitch ass out in the open, ole cockroach ass muthafucka!"

I looked around and the entire front room of the house was vacant. But the half-eaten plates of food still on the table, told me that we weren't alone.

"I know your ass up in here. Don't even think about tryin' to be brave, nigga!" I shouted as I walked around opening all the closed doors. "My niggas know where ya mammy stay!"

I heard Murk laughing from behind me as he kicked over a table and knocked shit off the walls.

"This muthafucka hidin', ole bitch ass nigga," he chuckled.

We ran up in the hall and kicked down the door of the first bedroom we walked into. It was the master but it was empty. I signaled quietly to Murk and we padded over to the other bedroom. He kicked open the door and we stormed in with our guns in the air.

We were on some stupid shit because a nigga could've really bust first on our asses but, to be honest, we weren't thinking too straight. We were on a 'kill or be killed' mission and, just as I always thought, if anything went down, it was just my time to go.

Peeking in the room, I saw a woman with her hair wrapped up in a scarf and tears streaming from her eyes, which were sprung wide open in fright as she held onto two children, a boy and a girl. Something about her horrified and haunted expression as she clutched her babies made me pause for a minute, and I was hit with an image of my own mother. I shook away the disturbing memory when I heard Murk open the closet door from beside us.

When I peered inside, I almost instantly burst out into laughter.

"Murk," I said as I eyeballed the corner of the small closet. "I know this nigga's bitch ass ain't hiding behind a fuckin' stuffed animal."

If I hadn't seen the shit with my own eyes, I wouldn't have believed it. I knew that Mello had gay ass niggas on his team but I wasn't prepared for this.

We had gotten word of where one of his lieutenants, Bean, lived with his baby mama, so we didn't waste time acting on the news. Bean was supposed to be a top-notch goon but here his bitch ass was in the corner of the closet in his kid's room, hiding behind a big ass teddy bear and wearing nothing but his damn drawers.

"Man, get your gay ass outta there," Murk ordered, kicking the teddy bear out the way and exposing Bean, who immediately put his hands in the air. He was shivering profusely, no doubt fully aware that he was living his last moments.

I sneered at his scary ass as he cowered in the corner. The fact that he had the audacity to have teardrops and shit tattooed on his face amazed me.

Fake ass thug.

"Legend! I ain't have nothing to do with that shit concerning your bitch! I swear, nigga, I ain't know shit!"

"Relax," I told him with ease. "I know you ain't have nothing to do with all that. You good, nigga. I just want you to deliver a message to Mello for me."

With that revelation, Bean's eyes lit up with hope at the chance of possible survival. Uninterested now that he knew Bean was a full-fledge pussy, Murk lowered his weapon, deciding that his full attention was no longer needed. Seeing him back down gave Bean even more hope that he had a chance to escape with his life.

"Man, I ain't have nothin' but utter RESPEK for you and your niggas! I swear I ain't have shit to do with your bitch!"

The side of my mouth twitched at him calling Shanecia a bitch once again and I felt my trigger finger flex. Just then, one of his children let out a loud wail from behind me, reminding me that they were still in the room watching everything.

"Get your stupid ass out that damn closet!" I ordered him.

With trembling knees, he obeyed without another word. I motioned with my gun for him to start walking out of the room and he did as I asked. But not before delivering a grim look to his baby mama and children. His woman opened up her mouth and let out a wail so full of emotion that it made me cringe. Why sensing her distress made me think of my own mother, I didn't know.

Following behind Bean as he dragged his feet along the dingy laminate floor, I guided him with my gun to the living room. Murk came up behind me, making sure to close the door to the children's room behind him in order to shield them from witnessing their father's tragic end. We were hood niggas but we still had a heart.

As soon as we got into the living room, Bean stopped but I had another idea.

"Walk out the door," I told him.

"W—wh—what?" he stuttered, his eyes raking back and forth between my face and Murk's.

I didn't say a thing as I glared back at him. Murk, now curious about what I had on my mind, walked up beside me and watched intently, waiting for what would come next.

Swallowing hard, Bean staggered towards the door, pausing only for a few seconds when he was right in front of it. I nudged him forward with the barrel of my gun and he grabbed the handle, then walked out.

The golden sun poured directly into my eyes as we ambled out in single file. I kept the barrel of my gun pointed right at Bean's back, nudging him whenever he began to slow down in pace. Dame and Quan turned towards us and then I saw their attention shift sharply to Murk, both set of eyes asking him the unspoken question: *What the hell is this nigga up to?*

Clueless, Murk shrugged and Quan shifted uneasily as his eyes peppered the nearly empty street. Some people were still outside scrutinizing our every movement and I knew many others were probably ogling curiously from their windows.

Good, I thought. *I need an audience.*

"Okay, nigga," I said, finally. "I told you I wanted you to deliver a message to Mello for me, right?"

Distraught nearly to the point of fainting, Bean nodded his head as much as he could. His quaking body was almost to the point that he could barely stand on his own two feet.

"Well, here is the message. I need you to repeat what I say exactly how I say it, got it?"

He nodded once again.

Leaning over, I spoke a few words into his ear. By the time I was finished, he looked like he was about to pass the fuck out. Shaking his head vigorously, he turned towards me with his eyes stretched so wide they were nearly protruding from the sockets.

"N—n—no, please, man! I s-s-s-swear I didn't—"

Growing impatient, I smacked him across the back of the head with my weapon. He was so afraid that he didn't even seem to register pain from the blow.

"Nigga, you supposed to be from the streets. Shut up all that blubbering and accept your muthafuckin' fate before I make it so it don't go down quite this easy, ya feel me?"

Catching my meaning, Bean clenched his jaw and turned away. He knew that I usually tortured niggas before they met their end. I was taking it easy on him and the best thing for him to do was to be gracious since I was being so merciful.

"Every day until—"

"*Louder!*" I pressed him.

"EVERY DAY UNTIL MELLO IS BROUGHT FORTH, SOMEONE WILL DIE! CONSIDER THIS DAY..."

"Muthafuckin'..." I coached.

"...CONSIDER THIS DAY MUTHAFUCKIN' ONE! D-BOYS FOR LIFE!"

As soon as Bean finished his announcement, a malicious grin crossed my face. Lifting my weapon, I aimed it at his neck. He squeezed his eyes closed and prepared for the kill shot.

POW!

Blood splattered as he dropped to the ground like a stone, his head partially severed from his body. I heard a shrill, agonizing scream from behind me and I knew it was his baby mama who we'd left inside. Stepping to the side, I allowed her access to mourn her sudden loss.

"Let's go," I told my brothers while trying my best not to look at the woman. "We're done here."

"See no evil, shawty," Murk told Bean's baby mama as she continued to wail.

Even in her distress, I knew she made sure to acknowledge her words. Everyone knew the consequences of talking to anyone about anything they'd seen us do. Especially the police.

My brothers all exchanged glances at each other as I walked away with ease, feeling a little lighter in spirit knowing that my full on assault against Mello had officially started. If he didn't show his face, his men would die and he would be proving to the hood that he was the coward I already knew he was.

When I sat down in the whip, I was hit with my reflection in the mirror. My face was covered with Bean's blood. I looked just like the savage I was. Lifting my hand, I mopped up the blood from my face, but ended up smearing it in the process.

"Fuck it," I muttered under my breath.

Murk, Damn and Quan piled in the car. No one said a word but they were giving off crazy vibes. Then finally Quan spoke up.

"That nigga bossed up at the end, huh? Took that kill shot like a man," Quan snickered as he tried, and failed, to lighten the mood. Resorting to humor was always his tactic when he was in an uncomfortable situation.

"That was some reckless shit you just did, Legend," Dame started, using a reprimanding tone. It was in these rare moments that I was reminded that he was the oldest of us all.

"We've bodied niggas in the open before but you know the rules… you gotta cover your face, nigga. These snitchin' ass muthafuckas out here got cellphones and will record every fuckin' thing. I can't have you catching no case out here," Dame continued.

"I don't give a fuck about no muthafuckin' case. If somebody wants to get bold and turn rat on a nigga, I'mma make an example out of that muthafucka too!"

My phone chimed and I grabbed it up as I continued to drive.

"Aye, I ain't got no issues bodying these coward niggas," Murk added, clicking his tongue against his teeth as he finger-fucked his gun.

"We already knowin' that shit, you crazy ass nigga," Dame replied, giving him a look. "But I promised mama before she died that I wasn't gonna let anything happen to her baby boys and—"

"Nigga, what?! We spend more time takin' care of you than you do us!" Quan interrupted, jabbing Dame in the side. "I love mama, but I don't know what the hell she was thinking trying to put your ass in charge of shit that don't involve pussy."

Murk snickered at Quan's statement and I couldn't help doing the same as I checked my message.

"It's because I'm most like her so she understood me best," Dame reasoned. "Me and mama...we both misunderstood. People like to say shit about us but, for real for real, we just got too much love to keep to ourselves so we spread it to everybody."

Reaching out, Quan punched Dame in the shoulder and sneered. "Man, is you trying to call mama a hoe?"

The vehicle went completely silent as we all pondered the answer to Quan's question. We all knew the truth—after my pops passed, she was pretty damn loose. But we had too much respect to actually say it.

All except for dumb ass Dame.

"Well, if y'all niggas ain't gone say it, I will," Dame finally spoke up while uncomfortably scratching at his clean-cut beard. "But if a chick like mama gave me her number...shiiiiiddd, I'd be scared as hell to holla. Ain't no tellin' what the hell she got going on between them—"

Murk leaned into the back seat from where he sat and both he and Quan started punching the shit out of Dame as he laughed and tried to block their hits. I would have joined in but I was preoccupied by the text message that I was looking at.

I had a few lined up but it was the one from Shanecia that caught my attention.

Lil Booty Girl: *I'm awake. Can you take me home?*

"SHIT!" I yelled, hitting a hard and very illegal U-turn in the middle of the four lane street. "Neesy's up!"

"Well, where the hell you takin' us?" Dame asked, frowning.

"To the fuckin' hospital! Where you think? I said Neesy's up," I repeated as I grew agitated by him asking questions he should have already known the answer to.

"Legend, look at yo' fuckin' face and your shirt! You think it's cool for you to walk in that shit covered in somebody's blood?"

I paused. He was right. It was true that I was getting careless but I couldn't be stupid.

"Quan, give me your shirt."

Without hesitation, he did as I asked and I swapped mine out for his while I continued to drive.

"Here," I muttered as I tossed my shirt back at him.

"No thanks," Quan quibbled as he threw the shirt behind him. "I'll pass on rocking a nigga's brains."

"And your face?" Dame asked me.

Looking up, I gazed into the rearview mirror. "It ain't that bad."

Murk started to chuckle as Dame shook his head and turned towards the window, giving up completely on trying to play the big brother role. At least he could say he tried.

Chapter Four

SHANECIA

I was just about asleep when I heard the door to my room burst open. In walked Legend wearing a tight expression on his face, which was smeared with a dried up, reddish substance.

"You good?" he asked me, his voice rugged but light at the same time.

Still distracted by his appearance, I nodded my head. "Yeah, I just feel a little dizzy. The nurse was just in here and she told me that I just need to drink a lot of fluid…and, of course she spoke to me about drug rehab." I snorted a laugh despite my situation. "She thinks I'm a junkie."

"Well, you O.D.'ed so she would think that. But you're good now. Get your ass up and let's go."

Put off by his rough temperament, I watched as he walked over to the small sink in the adjacent bathroom, wet a paper towel and started cleaning his face.

"Is that blood?" I asked him.

"Naw."

"Are you lying?" I pushed with a scowl.

"Yeah."

Hesitant, I bit my lip and pushed away the question I really wanted to ask: Was it Mello's? Although I was in a relationship with Legend, my values and his weren't the same. I didn't want to see anyone lose their life and I couldn't bear being the cause of it. But to know that Mello would no longer be a worry of mine or Tanecia's would be a blessing.

"Legend…D—did anyone tell you about Tan yet? She's in here, too. Darin says Mello shot her the same day he grabbed me. She's in ICU and they are saying she might not make it," I said, barely above a whisper.

Legend's body went rigid for less than a second before returning to normal. His reaction was so sudden that had I blinked at that exact moment, I would have missed it.

"I heard about Tan. If it's her time, it's her time. If not, she'll survive," was all he said using a flat tone.

Pushing the covers off my body, I tried to ignore the fury building up in my heart and bottle the words about to spill out of my mouth but I couldn't.

"Is that your version of offering me some encouragement? Let me repeat myself so you can catch what I'm saying this time. My *sister* is in ICU fighting for her life! She was shot TWICE!"

After throwing the soiled napkins into the trash bin, Legend walked over and looked me square in the eyes. There was an emotion hidden behind his pupils that I couldn't read, but I knew enough to understand that he expected whatever he was about to say to be the last few words spoken on the subject.

"You're not a little girl, Neesy. You're a grown woman who is datin' a street nigga and I'mma treat you as such. Your sister made a choice. She chose to fuck with a nigga who don't give a fuck about your life or hers, but she did it anyways. What happened to her was the consequence of a lifestyle *she* chose."

By the time he'd finished speaking, I felt like I did the day I'd heard him ordering his brother to grab a man who'd stolen money from him. I felt naïve and undereducated about the life I was now living as his girl. Was I choosing a similar path to Tanecia's by being with Legend?

He must have sensed my feelings because, all of a sudden, his demeanor changed and he started to look at me with a softer expression on his face.

"I'll protect you," he assured me softly. "You just got to trust me and listen to me. You have a tendency to be bull-headed and too emotional before thinking. Just let your nigga be your man."

The fire in me cooled down to a small flame, but I still felt angered about his view on Tanecia's survival. If it had been his family, I knew he would have a different take on it. Pulling my chin up, Legend caught my eyes and cradled them in his loving gaze. He relaxed me in an instant.

"I'll protect you always. But I'm not responsible for anyone but you and my blood. And I'm not even responsible for them if they choose the wrong path."

He paused when he said that and I had a feeling that there was something more behind that statement. But I didn't ask and he didn't explain further.

"Let's go," he said with a sigh. "I gotta get you home."

Chapter Five

MALIAH

The way my heart was pounding in my chest could barely be explained. I was nervous. I was excited. I was afraid. I had a million emotions going through my mind all at one time and I didn't know what to make of it. All I knew was that my life was about to change yet again and, for some reason, I was certain it wouldn't be for the best.

"Ma'am?" a nurse called, snatching me out of my daydream.

I looked up into her pleasant, cocoa-colored face and pressed my thick lips together as I tried to steady the rapidity of my pulsating heart.

"Yes?" I replied with a mousy voice.

"You may go in now. He's just been given some medication to ease his pain and it makes him a little drowsy so he may seem a little weak but that's just a side effect of the medicine. He's actually coming along quite fine," the middle-aged woman assured me.

I nodded my head and watched her turn around and walk down the hall before I stood up and exhaled sharply. Glancing towards Danny's room, I hesitated for only about a second before padding steadily towards the door.

This was a moment I never thought I'd see, and here it was. The man who I'd loved since the day I realized what love was, had been taken from me for what I'd believe would be forever, but here he was…still alive. I was living the storyline of your favorite soap opera.

Pushing open the door, I walked in and my eyes immediately fell upon Danny's frail body. He looked even thinner than he had before. Even with the bandages around his chest and stomach, he appeared so tiny under the bulky material.

"Li-Li…you came," he croaked, making me jump.

I was so focused on staring at his body that I didn't even realize his eyes were open and trained on my face. Licking my lips, I refocused my attention on his face and searched his eyes with mine. My heart warmed when I saw he was lucid and seemed well and healthy despite his injuries. His eyes were big, bright and white. He was far removed from the dope fiend I'd come to know him as.

"Of course," I replied, sitting in the chair at his bedside. I grabbed his hand and pulled it into mine. His skin was rough, dry and cold.

"I thought you were d—"

Suddenly stricken by superstition, I paused. I was unable to get the words to leave my mouth, as if admitting it would make them eventually come true.

"I thought you were gone," I finally admitted quietly.

"I know," he chuckled in a dry, forced way that made me tremor with the pain I'd imagined he probably felt. "I thought I was gone too. I'm sure everyone did. Truth is…I should have been but all them years of you praying for me…I—I think they finally came through."

My heart jumped in my chest and I swallowed hard. I couldn't ignore the love that I'd felt. The love I would always feel. I knew we couldn't be but I couldn't shake the fact that Danny and I had a bond that would never go away. It was far more than the children we shared.

Danny was the first man who made me feel loved. He was the first to make me feel like a woman. It hurt my heart that we couldn't be together because I knew it was the right choice but, even still, I wanted the best for him. The last thing I wanted to do was be caught up in between him and Murk.

Murk, I thought finally and then let my eyes fall over the bandages on Danny's chest where he'd been shot.

"What happened to you? Was it Mello?" I asked a leading question, hoping that he'd say it was. If Murk had shot him, I wasn't sure I could take it.

Danny's chapped lips parted slightly and his eyes pensively raised to the ceiling as he thought back in time. I could almost see the wheels in his head turning as he tried to bring back memories of the day that he'd almost died.

"I—I can't remember," he disclosed finally with the corners of his eyes tugging downward in sadness. "I was so fucked up after you left. Emotionally and physically. And…I—the only way I could think to cope was to—"

"You got high," I finished for him and angrily released his hand from mine. "And you were high when you got shot so you don't remember shit."

I could see the hurt in Danny's eyes as I started to get angry, but I couldn't help it. His little revelation pissed me off all the more and I didn't know if it was because I couldn't confirm for sure that Murk didn't have anything to do with him almost dying, or because I was being reminded that the love of my life and father of my children was nothing but a junkie.

"Li-Li…I'm not using that shit again, I swear. I know what it's done to our family and I promise I'm done," he promised me for the millionth time.

Infuriated, I stood up and aimed my eyes at him, shooting daggers of fury with each passing second.

"Do you know how many times you've told me that, Danny?!" I roared, louder than I'd initially intended.

Caught off guard by my sudden outburst, he looked directly at me with pleading eyes, his bottom lip wiggling as if he were trying to find something to say. I sensed movement behind me. When I whirled around, it was a mousy looking nurse walking in with her shoulders hunched over as if they were being used to shield her from my fury.

"Um…ma'am, you're going to have to quiet down or—"

Still incensed by my rage, I put my hand in the air to stop her.

"Don't bother, I'm leaving," I muttered.

She seemed more than happy to hear that I was leaving before she had to tell me to. With a small, awkward smile, she bowed out of the room.

Walking over to where I'd been sitting, I leaned down and grabbed my purse. When I stood up, Danny had sat up as much as he could on the bed, even though I could see it pained him to do so.

"Li-Li, don't leave yet. I'm sorry, baby. I promise that I'm done. I just want to be there for my children and for you."

"Danny, I don't need you to be there for me anymore. The kids need you but only if you get better. If you can't get it together for them then they will be better off without you," I snapped back at him.

Hurt, Danny flinched, and I could tell that my words were cutting him like a knife but I didn't care. After everything that I'd been through, he deserved to feel his share of the pain.

"Can you at least bring them to see me?" he asked pitifully in a way that tugged at my heart strings.

Pursing my lips, I tried to blink away the tears that were building up in my eyes. One lone tear escaped and I wiped it away as I shook my head sadly.

"I'm not going to bring them up here," I told him.

With a stricken look on his face, Danny gawked at me unbelievably.

"But my kids…think I'm dead, right? I need to—"

"If you don't get your life together, you *will* be dead to them," I replied honestly. "I'm finally doing what's right by my kids and I will not allow them to be around you with the life you're living."

Silence loomed as we sized each other up, Danny's eyes turning from soft to vicious in a matter of seconds. Suddenly, he opened his mouth and let out a callous, dry cackle.

"You are one to judge me for what I do when you out shaking your ass in the club every night."

My mouth dropped open as my cheeks began to heat up from embarrassment. I had no idea that Danny knew about my dancing. Suddenly, tears returned to my eyes as I began to get pissed off the more I thought about what he'd said. All this time and he still didn't get it.

"You're fucked up for that, D," I gritted through my teeth as the tears fell slowly down my cheeks. "I'm shaking my ass on the pole because *you* couldn't be the man I needed. I had to take care of *our* kids by myself because you'd rather trade your money for nose candy rather than feed ya fuckin' kids!"

Danny's expression shifted and I could see that he was beginning to understand the major error in his statement. He wanted to condemn me for stripping but he was the one who drove me to it.

"Li-Li, I'm sorry, I—"

"Save it," I mumbled.

With my bag tucked under my arm, I backed out of the room and walked out. Each step brought about a feeling of exhilaration and liberty from a situation that I should have ended a long time before.

By the time I hit the parking lot, I was positive that I'd made the right choice by leaving Danny right where he was. I was glad he was alive but I couldn't do that shit with him anymore. He wasn't ready to change and I couldn't allow him to take me and my children back to the hell he'd created for us.

And either way it didn't matter. I was with Murk now, and he was all the man I needed and more.

Chapter Six

LEGEND

Murk: *It's getting' harder to find these niggas. They hidin'.*

Gritting my teeth, I fought the urge to throw the phone across the room and pecked out a quick reply.

Pussy ass niggas.

It was day four of my assault on Mello and his bitch ass still hadn't shown his face yet. Just like I'd known, he was a bitch. What kind of leader would stand around and allow his men to get slaughtered in broad daylight? I never had respect for the nigga but I definitely wouldn't now. There was nothing honorable in being a man and acting like a pussy.

Now, his whole team was hiding so that we couldn't run up on them for fear that they would be the next example. All of the normal spots that they usually visited on the regular were no more. I had Murk on patrol to find one because we had about two hours until somebody had to get ready for their date with Mercy, my Desert Eagle.

Popping a pill in her mouth before taking a gulp of water, I eyed Shanecia as she walked by me wearing the shortest little dress I'd ever seen her in.

"What's that you takin'?" I questioned her with one eyebrow lifted. This wasn't the first time I'd seen her ass popping pills.

"The doctor gave me a prescription before I left the hospital. It was for pills…to treat anxiety. After everything that happened, I—I just needed something to calm my nerves and help me relax," she explained nonchalantly like it wasn't anything that she'd become a pill-popper overnight.

"Don't be takin' too much of that shit," I told her with the corner of my lip lifted in a sneer.

I didn't like the idea of no lady of mine taking anything that would affect her mood. It was too close to why fiends was usin' the shit I pushed on the streets. It was too easy to move from gettin' a legal high to an illegal one. But I dropped the subject for now and decided to continue watching her.

"How long I gotta wait until I can get up in that stomach again?" I asked.

Eyeballing her in that little ass dress, I made a mental note to snatch that shit up and hide it as soon as she took it off. She wouldn't be wearing that shit nowhere else for no other niggas to be looking at her fine ass. She'd mess around and show off them long ass legs around the wrong muthafucka, and I'd have to end up bodying a disrespectful nigga. Right now I had enough shit going on, I didn't need to add more bodies to the pile.

"Legend, why the hell you keep asking me that? It's only been two days since I been home! You act like you ain't had nothing in months!"

She blew out a breath as she flopped down on the couch across from where I sat. Her dress blew up slightly and I saw she wasn't wearing panties. Twisting up my lips at her, I stood up and walked over to where she stood. Here she was sitting across from me in a short ass dress with no panties on underneath and she thought I wasn't gonna hit. She had me fucked up.

"Stop playin' with a nigga. Take that shit off, ma," I ordered, standing over her.

Licking my lips, I smirked. I felt my man growing through my shorts the longer I eyed her legs, knowing that there wasn't anything in between me and the spot that I was craving. Nothing other than her stubborn ass attitude.

Shanecia sucked her teeth then rolled her eyes before crossing her legs, which gave me another peek at her pussy. It looked like she had just shaved it. Now she *really* had me fucked up.

"Legend, leave me alone! I just wanna read and relax. I don't feel like being bothered right now," she responded as she reached over and picked up her Kindle.

Annoyed, I swatted the shit right out of her hands, making her gasp all loud and dramatic like she was surprised.

"Neesy, you got me fucked up! Take that shit off and open your muthafuckin' legs so I can get some pussy. I got shit to do and you holding me up! I'm not finna play these bullshit ass games with you. You know you want this! Why you always gotta make a nigga beg for what's mine?"

Trying to hold back a smile, she rolled her eyes and twisted around to grab her Kindle from where it had landed. As soon as she reached over, I scooped her little ass up and threw her over my shoulder.

"LEGEND! Nigga, put me down!" she yelled. I didn't respond and before long, she was punching me in the back with her fists, like that shit was supposed to hurt.

"If this is how your ass planned on fighting the first time we met, I'm glad I let your ass go," I grumbled as she continued to wail off on me.

Walking to the long, formal dining room table with her still draped over one shoulder, I tugged her legs apart and stuck two fingers directly into her pussy and start pushing in and out as I used my thumb to caress her asshole. She relaxed instantly.

"Mmmmm, that shit feels good, baby," she cooed, opening her legs a little more to give me more access.

"You like that?" I asked with a smile on my face.

I started stirring her shit as it got wetter and wetter until it started smacking like macaroni and cheese. Licking my lips, I flipped her around so that her hands were rested on the table but her back end was elevated in the air. Grabbing her thighs, I placed them on either side of my head, resting them on my shoulders, and my mouth salivated as I stared at her pink cave positioned right in front of my face. She was dripping wet and panting in anticipation for what I was about to do to her. She should have been scared because my intentions were to wear her shit out to the point that she couldn't even walk.

"Fuck!" she screamed when I pushed my entire face into her pussy, totally swallowing up her clit.

Holding onto her hips, I dove all the way in, moving back and forth between her warm cave to her ass. She began to twerk on me and I slapped her backside hard to make her stop. When it came to what I did best, I had to let her know that she didn't control shit. She didn't run this, I did.

After I got her to the point that she was dripping wet, I pulled back and looked at her clit. It was so swollen that I could almost see it throbbing before my eyes.

Mission accomplished, I thought to myself as I looked at how fat it was.

Twisting her over, I placed her on her feet facing me. She grabbed on the table behind her to keep her balance. Her legs were trembling to the point that she could barely stand.

"A'ight," I said as I dropped my shorts to the floor.

My man was standing at full attention and pointed directly at her. She licked her lips slowly as she looked at me. Grabbing the back of her head, I guided her down to her knees gently and positioned her mouth right to him.

Perfection was the only way to describe her head game. It wasn't always that way. The first time she gave me head, she was pecking at my shit with her tongue like Woody the fuckin' Woodpecker. When I told her to suck on it slow, she could barely even take the dick and just teased the head.

Now she was slowly learning how to deep throat my dick and that shit drove me insane. That was the thing about Shanecia. She was stubborn but determined and she'd be damned if she let another bitch outdo her at anything.

"Shiiiiiiit, you gotta slow that shit down," I told her. She was making my toes curl but I wasn't ready to bust yet.

Smacking and moaning, she ignored what I was saying and kept going.

"Slow that shit down, Neesy!" I told her again but she only sped up even more.

Furious, I grabbed the back of her head and wrapped her hair around my fingers. Since she wanted to play, I was gonna play right along with her ass. Holding tightly to her hair, I started to control the motion, slamming her mouth further down on my dick before yanking her head back. I kept making her deep-throat the dick, slamming it down her throat and making her gag before pulling her back.

Suddenly panicked, she started trying to talk and started pushing hard on me, as she attempted to get away. And that's when I let up and slid all the way out of her mouth. She backed away, her eyes filled with fury and frowned up at me as she rubbed her throat.

"I told your ass that you don't run shit, I do!" I barked at her while stroking my rod.

I knew I was acting like an asshole because I was tense as fuck about the things happening in the streets. The hurt look in her eyes was fucking with me and it took everything in my power not to drop down, kneel in front of her and apologize. But Legend wasn't kneeling down to nobody, my lady or not.

Reaching down, I scooped her up in silence and laid her down on the table then started teasing her clit with the head of my dick as I watched her facial expression change. She still looked upset but after a while, I saw her bite on her lip and close her eyes. When our skin started smacking against each other from her juices, I slowly pushed in and slow-fucked her into ecstasy.

Leaning over, I continued pushing into her and planted a trail of kisses down her neck until I reached her breasts. She trembled and let out a sharp breath when I pulled her nipple into my mouth and started sucking on it gently as I continued to grind into her. I heard her gasp loudly in pleasure and it made me feel less fucked up about the way I'd treated her.

Right then, my goal changed and I was no longer seeking my own pleasure. I wanted to please her and, in doing so, I knew I would be satisfied. I bit gently down on her nipple and I felt her legs open wider, making my brow rise slightly. She liked a little pain with her pleasure. I liked that.

"Pleeeaaaase, don't stop," Shanecia begged as I continued to stroke inside of her.

She clenched her teeth together and I could tell she was trying her hardest not to take control of the movement and that made me smile. To see a woman like her who is always in control of everything decide to finally let go, was sexy to me. I needed her to relax when she was with me and she was starting to learn.

Lifting her legs higher until her calves were rested on my shoulders and her feet were up in the air, I sped up faster and faster. She gritted her teeth and grabbed the edge of the table, taking that shit like a pro as I pushed further and further into her. Soon, her legs were trembling and her body was jerking. I increased my motion, and then slid out a little before pressing my thumb down hard on her button. A grin rose up on my face when she started squirting all over the damn place.

"Ugggghhhhh, shitttttttttt!" she yelled so loud that she had my fuckin' ears ringing, as she writhed on the table under my touch. I pressed harder on her clit and she squirted a few more times before her body went limp.

"What the fuck?!" she shouted, nearly breathless once she'd come down from her high.

Leaning up, Shanecia looked at the wet spots she'd made all over the table and on my t-shirt.

"Yo' juicy ass just squirted," I laughed while staring at the bewildered look on her face.

"I what?!"

"You just squirted…you ain't never heard of that shit before?"

Her silence was the answer to my question and I just shook my head, then pulled my shirt from over my head.

Throwing it at her, I smirked and started to laugh.

"Clean up the table, nigga. Yo' nasty ass done squirted that juice all over my shit. Now a nigga can't even eat a damn meal without thinkin' about that pussy."

Rolling her eyes, Neesy stood up with her legs wide as if she was afraid to let the sweet nectar on her thighs touch.

"It ain't like you ever stop thinking about it anyways," she replied cockily while sucking her teeth.

"You right."

Walking back into the living room, I grabbed my phone and checked my messages. There was nothing else from Murk and it was starting to piss me off.

Grabbing up Mello's niggas wasn't working, so I had to take it a step further. If these niggas weren't going to help me flush his bitch ass out, my next step was to start grabbing up their women.

Touching families usually went against my personal rules but all that was out the window the second they'd laid hands on my lady. They had to learn that wasn't nothing off limits when it came to what I needed to do in order to get what I wanted.

Chapter Seven

MURK

Yeah, I was supposed to be on my way to meet up with Legend but the way that Maliah was walking around swinging that big ole booty of hers was posing a fuckin' problem. Instead of walking my ass out the house, getting in the car and going to meet up with my brother, I was laid back in my recliner with my hands behind my head and watching her on her hands and knees while she colored on the floor with the kids.

She had on some lil' ass jean shorts on and I *knew* she had to know a nigga was looking. Otherwise, why the hell was she all booted over and shit with her back arched and her ass up? There wasn't a damn thing they were coloring on that ugly ass sheet of paper that required all that extra shit she was doing.

"YAY, Dej, you stayed in the lines!" she leaned up and started clapping while bouncing up and down which made her ass jiggle.

A smirk crossed my face as I stared at the juicy piece of meat that was making its way out of the too-small shorts she was wearing. My dick started to get hard in my pants the more I looked at it. Yeah, I needed to go but right now what I really needed was Maliah.

"Aye, c'mere girl," I commanded her as I ran my tongue over my teeth with my eyes still planted on her ass.

She turned all the way around, giving me a full view of her fat kitty. I heard her suck her teeth so I reluctantly pulled my eyes up so that I could look at her in the face.

"For real, Murk?" she said like she was annoyed but I knew she liked that shit.

"I need you to take care of somethin' real quick," I told her and grabbed at my hard dick. "They ain't lookin'!" I said when I saw her head shoot around to look at the kids.

"Yeah, but all of their asses are wide awake! You can't wait until you come back home?"

"Hell naw," I replied with a frown as I eyed her up and down. "If you wanted me to wait, you shouldn't have come out in that itty, bitty shit you got on!"

Sucking her teeth again, she turned back around to the kids and then grabbed the remote to turn the TV on.

"I'm going to go…read Murk a story real quick," she lied. "Y'all stay in here and watch TV. I'll be back."

Maliah stood up and walked over to me then grabbed my hand. I followed her back to the room, keeping my eyes on her ass the whole way, as it swished from side-to-side.

"That was a dumb ass lie you told them," I chuckled as soon as we got into the room. Closing the door behind me, I pulled off my t-shirt.

"Well, what the hell you wanted me to say?" Maliah asked me. She licked her lips as she stared at my body. She always tried to act like she ain't wanna give me the pussy, but she was even more of a freak than I was. I loved that shit too.

"Hell, I don't know but I don't want Jari growing up thinkin' that I be 'round here gettin' stories read to me and gettin' tucked in and shit like I'm a lame ass nigga! I lay dis dick down and then I put your ass to sleep! That's what he needs to know because that's what da fuck be happenin' in here!"

Rolling her eyes, Maliah dropped to her knees right in front of my erection and started unbuckling my jeans.

"Jari is barely one-year-old. He is not worried about what you be doin' in here," she opined with a tone that suggested I was being ridiculous.

"Well, tell that nigga that we walkin' back here so I can do some manly shit like change a lightbulb or something. Don't have that nigga thinkin' I'm listening to your ass tell me a gotdamn sto—SHIT!" I cursed loudly when Maliah sucked my entire dick in between her jaws.

Wrapping her hand around the base of it, she shoved it further and further down her throat just like the pro she was. That shit felt so good that she had me seeing muthafuckin' stars. Pulling back, she spit on it before sucking it back in her mouth. I loved when she got nasty with me.

"Damnnnn, Maliah!"

I almost bust instantly when she deep-throated me so far down her throat that her damn tonsils seemed to be tickling my balls. Her head game was *the shit*! I wouldn't tell her that, because I knew she would get the big head, but there wasn't a chick I'd ever been with who could do it the way that she did, and that was saying a lot. A lot of bitches had tried swallowing my entire dick and failed. But Maliah was up to the challenge from jump and after some practice, she was able to swallow it all.

She started squeezing my shaft with her hand and sped up the motion. Leaning back, I put my hand on the dresser behind me and started pumping into her mouth as she worked it faster and faster, sucking harder with every second. I felt the nut build up inside me and I knew it was about to happen…I was about to cum.

Reaching out, I grabbed the back of her head and thrust one more time into her mouth. She responded by doing some shit where it felt like her throat was closing in around my dick and became tight, as she tickled the tip of my head with her tongue. That was exactly what I needed. Gritting my teeth, I let go and dumped what felt like a gallon of my hot liquid straight down her throat. She swallowed it all… down to the last drop.

I love her ass, I thought to myself as I watched her stand up and wipe at the side of her mouth before dipping her fingers inside to lick off anything that hadn't made it inside.

"You nasty as fuck!" I told her, watching her walk into the bathroom to clean up.

"Yeah, but you love that shit," she said.

Laughing, I nodded my head. She was absolutely right.

"Aye, when you gone quit your job at the club?"

I walked in the bathroom behind her while wiping off my dick with one of DeJarion's wet wipes that were in the room. She glanced at me before continuing what she was doing.

"I want to save up enough money to where I feel comfortable quitting first," she said simply.

I frowned and leaned back on the door. "You know who the fuck you dealin' with, right? You act like whatever you need, I can't handle!"

"I know you can handle it, Murk," she said rolling her eyes. "I just don't *want* you to. I want to have my own money and be able to depend on myself for a change!"

"Yeah, a'ight," I replied as I tossed the wet wipe in the trash. "I gotta meet up with my brothers. I'll be back later."

She mumbled something that sounded like 'goodbye' but by that time, I was already pulling my shirt over my head and heading out the door.

"Yo," he repeated, jabbing me in the leg hard with his thick, grease-covered finger. "I *said*, do you got an attitude?"

"Damn, Legend, that hurt!" I rubbed at the spot on my leg that was still throbbing from his heavy-handed touch. "And no I don't have an attitude. I'm tired!"

"You always tired and you always eatin'. You was tired last night too, when I tried to get some," he shot at me while thinking back. "Matter of fact, don't even think of trying that shit tonight because a nigga is prepared to gorilla that pussy if you try to hold back, ya heard me?"

Gasping, I shot my eyes behind us to the older black women who were sitting right behind us. They were trying their hardest to avoid my eyes but I could tell they heard every damn word that he'd said.

"I can't believe you said that!" I groaned, partially covering my face with my hands. It felt warm under my fingers. I was mortified.

"Listen…I keep telling you. This is an important time for us to look strong." He leaned over so that his words could only be heard by my ears.

So now *this nigga wanna whisper,* I thought, rolling my eyes.

"There is a lot going on that you don't know about and it ain't good. You sense the vibe in here?"

He paused and I took a minute to contemplate on his words. Something had seemed off as soon as we walked into the rec center, but I was so caught up in my own feelings that I hadn't paid all that much attention to it.

Normally when we walked in, it was the cue everyone needed to really get the party started, but this time there was a bleak vibe in the air. People were watching and whispering amongst themselves but it wasn't like normal.

Everyone seemed to grow quiet as we passed by and the men went out of the way to make sure they paid homage to Legend as he passed by. I was also suddenly aware of the fact that the rec center was packed full of members of Legend's street team and they were all packing heat. I didn't know what he was doing on his end to make things change so suddenly, but whatever it was had the whole hood shook.

Curiosity piqued, I nodded my head softly and turned my attention to him so he could continue.

"What I need is for you to just stick with me for a few hours. The hood is talking about what happened with you and Mello. They expect you to be weak but you—"

"Gotta be strong when they expect you to be weak," I finished, then sucked my teeth and flipped my eyes to the ceiling as I scoffed. "I don't see what I have to do with all this. I'm just—"

"You're my lady and you rollin' with a fuckin' legend," he reminded me cockily. He lifted his head and peered down at me from the side of his eyes.

"You better stop whining and get some of my thug up in you so you can ride this thing out."

Snickering, I rolled my eyes and grabbed my phone. I wanted to check with Darin to see if there was any change in Tanecia's condition. As soon as we left from the rec center, I planned on convincing Legend to let me drive over there so I could see her.

A few minutes passed before the announcer began to speak and the game began. Seconds later, Murk strolled in but when I saw DeJarion sitting on his shoulders, I had to do a double-take.

"Check this nigga out," a humored voice said from behind me. It was Quan. I hadn't even realized that he and Dame had snuck in and sat right behind us.

"The family life looks good on 'im," Legend chimed in with his approval, while nodding his head as he watched Murk stroll towards us.

"Shiiiiid," Dame replied, scratching at his jaw. "The family life gonna start looking good on me too. Look…he got all the bitches slobbering over his ass and all he had to do was bring in a shorty."

I rolled my eyes at Dame's comment. He was such a pussy hound and it was sad as hell because any time anyone mentioned his chick he started acting all butt-hurt. I hadn't met Trell yet and I wasn't sure if it was because Dame never invited her anywhere or because she just didn't want to come. Either way, I couldn't wait for the day that I'd meet the woman who managed to have Dame's heart without being able to fully possess his body.

"Aye, y'all," Murk greeted everyone before sitting down.

He pulled DeJarion from his neck and sat him in-between him and Legend. Frowning, Legend gave Murk a look that bordered disgust and I had to catch myself before I slapped him in the back of his head.

"I don't do tots, my nigga," Legend announced as he scooted away from DeJarion who was reaching out to him with his slobbery fingers.

Amused by his reaction, Murk reached out and gave Legend a soft push on the shoulder. "Get used to it, bro. You and Neesy might decide to terrorize us one day with a little Leith."

I couldn't help smiling at the way Murk teased Legend because I knew it ticked him off every time someone mentioned his government name.

"Pablo, I done told you 'bout using my muthafuckin'—"

"Pablo?" I blurted out, scrunching up my face. A sheepish expression crossed Murk's face and he shrugged.

"My mama said my daddy might've been Dominican," he explained. DeJarion made a grunting sound and we all looked down at his face which was screwed up so tight, his cheeks were turning red.

"Pablo, look like your shorty 'bout to blow," Quan chuckled. "Better run and dangle his lil' ass over the toilet before he—"

"LET ME GO! LET ME GO!"

The players immediately stopped playing and the rec center went completely silent. Everyone turned their attention to the entrance where a woman was struggling to be freed from two other women who were trying with all their might to hold her back.

The woman was fairly small in stature but was thick with wide hips and large breasts. She had meaty arms that looked as if they could pack a mean punch. From the look of her tight fists balled up at her side, if the two women holding onto her didn't back down, they would soon find out.

"GET OFF OF ME NOW! He killed my daughter! I know he did!"

A sharp sensation traveled down my spine and a salty taste built up on my tongue when I saw her point a single, trembling finger towards Legend. Along with every other person in the center, I rotated my eyes to look at him but he appeared to be completely at ease, watching the woman while still absentmindedly shoveling fries in his mouth. Reaching down, he dropped the empty fry container between his feet and then grabbed his soda, taking a long swig, with his eyes still on the woman ahead of him.

"HE KILLED HER! I know he did! LET ME GO!"

The infuriated woman continued to struggle. The more she did, the stronger she seemed to get and the weaker the other women beside her appeared. Reaching out, I grabbed Legend's arm, wanting to ask him if what she was saying was true, but not sure I wanted to hear an answer that I wouldn't be able to live with.

"Legend, this ole girl's mama, right?" Murk asked, pointing at the woman. "Ole girl from the trunk?"

"Yessir," he mumbled.

Stuffing his hand into his pocket, he pulled out a pack of Skittles and popped some in his mouth. Astonished, my mouth fell partially open as I regarded his careless attitude. This woman was going crazy about the loss of her daughter...a girl *he'd* most likely murdered, and he didn't even seem to give a damn. Much like the time when I'd confronted him about my own mother.

"Legend—"

I stopped short when he raised his hand up to silence me. Frowning, I tried to ignore the anger rising up in me. But I knew all eyes were on us so it was not the time for me to be going off.

"LET GO!" the woman yelled one final time. It was at that moment that she was finally able to break loose.

With lightning speed, Murk grabbed up DeJarion who was happily gnawing on his fingers, and pushed him towards me. A puff of stinky air flew up from his soiled diaper, only momentarily distracting me from the sight of Murk reaching behind him to pull out his piece.

The woman's thunderous stomps echoed through the entire center as everyone watched, barely breathing, and wondering what in the world was going to happen next.

"Slow yo' roll, mama," Murk warned her with his hand out. Dame and Quan stood on either side of him, creating a wall between her and Legend who was nonchalantly scrolling through his phone.

"YOU KILLED HER, DIDN'T YOU?! Tell me! Just let me bury my baby!" she screamed in agony but kept her feet planted firmly in place. With all three brothers in front of her, holding weapons, she knew better than to test them any further.

With a hand full of Skittles, Legend stood up slowly and turned towards the distraught woman who was watching him with puffy, red and traumatized eyes. My chest tightened as I witnessed her anguish. I couldn't take too much more of this show but when I saw the fire in his eyes, I knew I better not do a damn thing or Legend would probably throw my ass in the same trunk he'd thrown this woman's daughter in.

"Murk," Legend called out.

Murk turned and Legend caught his eye, delivering an unspoken signal and my heart clenched in my chest. I'd seen them signal to each other plenty of times and it was never good.

With his banger still tucked at his side, tightly wrapped in his fingers, Murk casually side-stepped the woman whose total focus was on Legend, and began to walk out of the center. The only sounds you could hear was the heavy breathing of the distressed mother and Murk's heavy footsteps as he made his exit. Everyone was staring in anticipation of Legend's next move and their expressions were every bit as shocked as mine.

"You know who I am?" Legend asked, finally stuffing the Skittles back in his pocket. He straightened up his back, extending his already tall frame, so that it became even more blaringly obvious how much he towered over, not just the woman, but his other brothers.

"I d—do," the woman stuttered a response. Her shoulders slumped and her bottom lip began to tremble as Legend focused his piercing stare on her large frame. She curled her body inward as if she were trying to shrink away from him.

Please don't do anything to this woman, Legend, I begged him in my mind, hoping that he could pick up on my thoughts telepathically.

"Do you know who she is?" Legend asked.

Frowning slightly at his words, I was first confused but then shocked when I saw him turn slowly and point in my direction. My eyes slid from him back over to the woman who was staring at me with her sad, red eyes drooping down at the corners. Her mouth began to move as she worked up her response.

"Yes…th—that's your girlfriend?" she said more like a question than a statement.

"That's my woman," Legend corrected her. "Fucking with her is like fucking with me—"

"But I didn't—" the woman interjected.

"Your daughter did," he replied with a pointed look.

I felt my cheeks heat up as people began to stare at me and whisper. Most of them knew me as the woman who they'd seen with Legend but he was making them regard me in a different light. He was letting it be made known that the same respect they gave him should be given to me.

In the light of Mello's attack, he must have thought it was necessary to send a reminder that he was still *that nigga* and anyone who messed with his woman would meet the same fate he'd eventually bring to Mello.

Just then, the front doors to the rec center creaked open and everyone turned towards the sound. There, at the entrance, was Murk holding the end of a rope that was wrapped around the wrists of a young woman who I recognized instantly. She was the chick who had been eyeing me and Legend the first time he'd brought me to the rec center. Though she was alive, she was not in good condition at all.

The girl was dressed in worn, filthy clothes that looked like she'd been wearing them for weeks. Her weave was matted and filled with all kind of debris it had collected during the time she'd been away. Looking at her, you'd think she'd been sleeping under a bridge for a month. She must have stunk to high heaven because everyone they passed would turn up or cover their noses, making repulsive faces, as soon as the wind hit them.

"MY BABY! OH GOD, she's not dead!" the woman exclaimed thankfully before turning and running towards where her daughter stood on shaky legs.

"Mama?" the girl whispered in a raspy tone.

Her mother got to where she was and just about dived on top of her, knocking her to the ground as she grabbed her into a tight hug. Her daughter winced, probably from pain, as her mother gripped her tightly as if she never wanted to let go, while tears ran down her cheeks.

"Consider yourself lucky," Legend's voice boomed throughout the center as everyone watched the mother and daughter's tearful reunion.

Their cries of joy were cut short as soon as he began to speak. The mother turned around and settled her haunted eyes on Legend's stone cold face. Her daughter cast a wary glance at the ground, unable to force herself to look at him directly.

"She's alive but the next time someone fucks with mine, I won't be so nice," Legend said. "And if I find out that any of you know something about someone who fucked with mine, you'll meet the same fate as that muthafucka."

He swooped his pointed icy stare around the court at everyone sitting in the bleachers. Many ducked their heads to avoid his gaze, afraid of being called out for any reason.

Once he finished, he signaled to the referee to get the game started, pulled out his bag of Skittles and shoved some in his mouth before walking back over to where I sat, quiet as a church mouse.

The players began to jump right back into the game and the woman slipped out of the rec center, holding her daughter in her arms. Before long, people were jeering and carrying on as if nothing had happened when Omega sunk a basket from nearly half court. He'd quickly become the star of the team.

"Aye, where is Alpha?" Dame asked suddenly.

"I ain't heard from that nigga in a few days. Might need to check in," Murk replied as he plucked DeJarion from my arms and then took off towards the bathroom to change him.

Taking a deep breath, I peeked at Legend from the corner of my eyes before turning to look at him full on. His eyes were on the game but I could see his mind wasn't in it.

"You good?" he asked me before I could say anything. Slowly, I nodded my head.

"I was actually going to ask you the same."

"I'm peachy," he replied, nonchalantly.

I cut my eyes at him before sucking my teeth. The word 'peachy' didn't even sound right coming out his mouth but I let it go because I knew what his problem was. Mello had gotten to me and still he was unable to pay him back for what he'd done. Things would be off with him until he got that out of his system and I had to get used to it.

Especially since I had a feeling that the little incident that had happened at the rec center today wouldn't be the last glimpse I would get of Legend's thuggish ways.

Chapter Nine

MALIAH

"Shawty, we got beef?" Murk asked me when he walked into the house.

I cut my eyes at him and then shoved some food into DeJarion's mouth, as he slammed the door and stomped into the dining room where I sat. Shadaej and LeDejah waved happily at Murk before returning their attention to their food.

"No, whatchu think we got beef for?" I inquired playing dumb.

I knew exactly what his issue was. He'd been texting me all morning and I hadn't answered one message. Yes, I was wrong as hell for that, but I was pissed off that he was acting like he didn't know why I wasn't answering his messages.

The day before, he came home from the rec center with DeJarion, took a nap, and then left before I went to work. He hadn't come home at all that night and hadn't even given me an explanation as to why.

Then around 10 AM this morning, he texted me 'good morning' like his ass didn't owe me an explanation for being out all damn night.

"What the fuck you mean 'what I think we got beef for'?" he asked, pushing me hard in the head with his stiff, index finger. "You ain't answer yo' muthafuckin' phone all morning, that's why. You sure you wanna play this game with a nigga like me?!"

Frowning up at him, I handed DeJarion the spoon so he could feed himself, and then stood up with my arms crossed in front of me.

"Don't be cussing in front of my kids!"

"Cussing?!" he gawked at me like I'd grown a second pair of eyes. "Cussin' should be the least of your worries! You lucky I don't mop the floor with your ass right now! Why the hell you ain't answer the fu—why you ain't been answerin' the damn phone, Li-Li?!"

Briefly caught off guard, I wanted to laugh at the way he stopped himself before dropping the f-bomb in front of the kids. He was pissed and still doing what I'd asked but I was too furious to even fully appreciate that.

"You didn't come home all last night! That's why I didn't answer your calls or messages. Where were you, Murk? You don't think I deserve an explanation?"

A few seconds dragged by with the only sound being the noise the kids were making as they ate in silence behind us. Then his hazel eyes narrowed in on me for a tick longer before he answered my question.

"Nope," was all he said. Instantly I was enraged and wanted to slap him upside the back of his head, but he stormed away before I could.

With my fingers pinching the bridge of my nose, I waited for a few minutes to try to calm myself down before I stomped off behind him, leaving the kids eating their food quietly as if nothing was happening around them. They were used to living in a dysfunctional home but I had hoped that moving in with Murk would have put all that behind me.

When I walked inside the living room and saw Murk's ass relaxing in his black leather recliner with his feet up, I got mad all over again. The nerve of his ass!

"So you trying to tell me that if I went to the club for work and didn't come back all night or tell you where I was, you would be cool with that?"

Standing right next to him, I didn't even flinch when Murk cut his smoldering eyes in my direction.

"Yo, kill that shit, Li. Don't get yo' ass fucked up 'round here," he replied with ease.

As if to further illustrate his point, he reached behind him and pulled out his glock and sat it casually on his lap. Pursing my lips, I glared at him.

"So you can do whatever the hell you wanna do but if I do it, then I'mma get fucked up? How is that fair, Murk?"

"Listen, Maliah," he started in a tone so icy that I almost backed away from him when he sat up and looked me directly in my eyes.

"You ain't my bitch so you can't tell me what the fuck to do or when to do it. I got feelings for your ass so I'mma take care of you but that's it. Don't get this shit twisted and think you can start clocking a nigga. I goes wherever the fuck I want to go and ain't shit nobody gone say about it."

Tears came to my eyes and my lips started to tremble but I blinked them back quickly. I'd be damned if I let another nigga see me cry.

"That said, I'm also paying for everything in this bitch. You try me like I'm a fuck nigga and I'mma fuck yo' ass up. Choice is yours," he finished simply before laying back on the recliner with his hands behind his head.

Unbelieving of the way he was acting, I just stared at him for a few minutes, waiting for him to say that he was kidding or to take it all back, but he didn't. The tears came back so I stormed away and down the hall before he could see them fall from my eyes.

After crying my heart out into my pillow, I drifted off into sleep and woke up hours later to the sound of my phone chiming right next to my head. Groaning heavily, I rubbed at my swollen eyes and tried to ignore the metallic taste in my mouth as I checked the message. It was a number I didn't recognize.

Li-Li, this Danny. I been released and I promise I'm gettin my shit together. I ain't been using since that day. I know you don't believe me but I swear Ima be good for you and my kids.

Letting out a breath, I locked my phone and dropped it on the nightstand beside my bed without replying.

"Who was that?" a voice said from behind me.

When I turned around in the bed, Murk was standing at the doorway. Instantly, I felt my heartbeat speed up although he didn't seem to be upset or anything other than curious.

"It was Neesy," I lied.

"Oh," was all he said. An awkward look crossed his face as he scratched at his low-cut beard that sat perfectly against his chiseled jaw-line.

"Me and the kids watching movies and shit. You wanna come in here?" he asked in a way that seemed like it was his way of trying to make amends.

Sighing, I checked the clock on the nightstand before shaking my head softly.

"I gotta get ready to get them together so I can drop them off before I go to work," I replied.

"You still don't get this shit, do you?" Murk asked. I was confused by his question.

When I looked back up at his face, he looked livid. Then, in less than a second, his expression went blank but the callous and intense glimmer in his eyes remained. Something was wrong and I could feel it. The mood had shifted suddenly but I didn't know why. Staring at him, I probed his eyes in an attempt to figure out what I'd done wrong.

"Do what you gotta do," he replied. "I won't be here by the time you make it back."

And with that, he turned around and walked away, slamming the door behind him and leaving me wondering what the hell was really going on with him.

Chapter Eight

SHANECIA

Since the day I officially became Legend's lady, we'd gone to the rec center every week and even though I wasn't feeling my best, he made it clear that this week was no different. All I really wanted to do was sleep and eat but he kept telling me that I had to appear strong when others expected me to be weak. I was so tired of hearing that shit.

"You look good in them jeans," Legend told me while licking his lips, once we sat down on the bottom bleachers. "Yo' ass been eatin' like a horse but you still keepin' that shape."

"Mm hmm," I grumbled out a response while cutting my eyes at him.

About five seconds passed of him staring a hole into the side of my head before I turned to look at him with a wide-eyed expression on my face, as if to ask what he was looking at.

"Yo, you got an attitude?" he asked with his brows pulled into a tight scowl as he shoved a handful of fries in his mouth.

My lips curled up at the edges while I watched him chomp on the fries like they were the best meal in the world as he waited for me to respond.

Chapter Ten

SHANECIA

"Legend, why you always act so rude with me all the time?" I asked him just out of the blue as we sat in the living room letting the TV watch us.

I was reading my favorite book in the entire world, *Beloved* by Toni Morrison, while Legend messed around with his phone. With everything that was going on in my life, I needed some relaxation time and some normality. However, the character Paul D made me think about Legend the more I read the book.

"Rude?" he asked with one eyebrow lifted in the air. "I'm not rude. So what I mention your big ass head from time-to-time? That don't give you the right to call me rude!"

Rolling my eyes, I sat up and dropped the book down on my lap.

"See? That's what I mean. Why you can't just be sweet with all the insults?"

He looked at me like I had five eyeballs planted in my forehead.

"Listen...have you ever read this book?" I waved the book in the air. Legend read the title and then gave me a look as if to ask "You for real?". I sighed and started to explain it to him.

"Paul D is the main character's man in the book. He was a slave at this place called Sweet Home and he suffered so much there that he developed…issues. He tries not to become too attached to anyone and he has issues really showing his love to Seth—"

"The next time you're wonderin' why the hell I'm so rude, remember this shit, Neesy," he cut in. He dropped his chin into his hand and gave me an uninterested look.

"Anyways," I rolled my eyes. "He represses memories of his troubled past and since he won't deal with them, it causes issues in his relationship. He loves Seth but can't really be what she needs him to be."

When I said that last part, Legend squinted his eyes at me and pointed his index finger into his chest.

"I'm not the man you need me to be, Neesy? That's what you tryin' to say?" he asked me.

"Legend, out of *all* that I said, that's the only thing you wanna focus on?" I questioned him.

He just stared at me without blinking as if he were waiting for me to say that he was all the man I ever needed. I picked up my book and laid back down so I could continue reading. I was so done with his ass.

"You just need to read the book," I grumbled before I started back reading. He grunted his response.

Thirty minutes later, I was struck with another question and, although I knew it was probably too soon after my other one to ask, I couldn't help it.

"Remember when you said you 'don't do tots'? Does that mean you don't want kids one day?"

As soon as I asked, Legend's body seemed to go rigid. His reaction confused me. It was such a simple question but he seemed to be so put off by it.

"I ain't good with kids," was all he said.

"How would you know if you never had any?" I asked him. "Wouldn't you like to have a family one day? You never talk about your mama or your daddy but I'm sure you'd want a family of your—"

"Neesy, why the hell you keep askin' me all these damn questions?!" he yelled before kicking at the remote that had fallen on the floor. It went sailing across the room before cracking into the wall across from where we sat. Frowning at him, I turned back to my book.

"Rude," I muttered. "Just like I said."

He'd not only proven my point from earlier but also managed to piss me all the way off. What kind of relationship could you have with someone if they got upset about the simplest things?

A few minutes later, I heard him sigh and stand up. He walked up next to where I was sitting on the sofa and sat down, moving my legs into his lap.

"You remember when you came to me about your mama the first day I saw you?"

I nodded my head. Of course, I did.

"I spared your crazy ass for two reasons. Number 1, you were wearing a Spelman shirt and, although I knew you were from the hood, I could see you ain't have no street sense so you ain't know what the hell you were really doin'. Number 2…" His voice faded away and I could see he was struggling to get his words out.

"Number 2…my mama was hooked on drugs, too. After my daddy died, my stepfather was…killed."

The way he said 'killed' let me know there was more to the story.

"We left Louisiana and moved to Ft. Lauderdale but she had to hide her identity so we lived off the radar. She did little odds and ends jobs…got paid under the table. My brothers and I were bad asses so we stole shit and got in whatever trouble we could. All of us lived in a one-bedroom apartment in the hood. We made it however we could. Most days we ain't even have shit to eat. We didn't even go to school…everything we learned was self-taught.

I have another older brother, Quentin. He started selling drugs and shit to get by, but the rest of us weren't feeling that. It seemed like too much work when all we had to do was bust a nigga over the head and take *their* shit. Then one day my mama came home crying because she couldn't provide for all of us. We were getting evicted and had nowhere to go. Because of what happened to my stepfather, she couldn't even contact her own family for help. It fucked me up to see her like that..."

By this time, I was so caught up in the story that my mouth was wide open as I listened. I was just about living off of every word that came out of his mouth. Legend took a minute to collect himself before he began again.

"Me, Murk, Dame and Quan left to go steal whatever we could to help her get the money. When we got back with the cash, she was knocked out in the bed and I thought she was sleep...but she wasn't. Weeks went by and she started changing...the same way your mama had changed. She was addicted to drugs but we didn't know it at the time. It took a minute but I finally found out it was my fuckin' brother, Quentin, who gave her the first hit. He's the one who got her addicted and had some fucked up reason...said he was only tryin' to make her feel better about our shitty situation.

She was never the same from then on. Then one day she didn't have money for dope so she tried to steal from her dealer. He found her and killed her...my brothers and I were teenagers by this time. We found out who he was. I handled the dealer and then we took his money and product and learned the game. That's how we came out on top and fell into this life."

My entire mind was blown by the time Legend finished talking. His revelation about his childhood was like something I could have never in my life imagined. As much as I was a product of the hood, I was realizing how much my mother had sheltered me before she became addicted to drugs. I wasn't exposed to anything close to what Legend and his brothers went through.

"What happened with your brother, Quentin?" I asked.

"Fuck that nigga for life..." Legend spat angrily. "After we found out what he did to my mama, I swear I wanted to kill that nigga but Quan stopped me and let him leave. If I *ever* see his ass again, his ass is getting blasted on sight. I was 14 years old the last time I saw him but I'm not that old anymore and Quan can't stop me from doin' shit."

I retreated into my thoughts and tried to imagine how I'd feel if Tanecia had gotten mama hooked to drugs. I could understand Legend's reaction. It was bad enough to me that she'd been around when Mama got addicted, but to be the one who actually gave her the first hit? Yeah, I would be done with her ass too.

"I don't want kids because I'm not ready. My life is fucked up now because of what I went through. I don't want my kids living this life with me. All this shit I'm doin' now would have to stop before I even think about bringin' someone else into this world. Don't need another lil' Legend walkin' around this shit I got going on. It's not right. Not for my shorty," he said softly.

It was crazy that in all the time that we'd been together, I was finally feeling like I was getting a glimpse into his soul. He was at his most vulnerable moment and I was lucky enough to be the one he'd chosen to share it with.

"Me and my niggas ain't rude either," he told me, giving me a sideways look. "Quan gets through rough shit by tellin' jokes and shit. Dame gets through everything by…well, by fuckin'. Murk and I are the most alike because…our stepfather taught us at a very young age that it wasn't beneficial to us to have feelings." He clenched his teeth and looked away.

Crinkling my brows, I was just about to ask him to explain but he put his hand up to stop me.

"And before you ask, that's all I got to say about that shit."

Legend leaned over and gave me a deep kiss on the lips, flicking his tongue inside my mouth in the process. I was dripping wet and aching for him by the time he was done. He pulled away and I knew he could see it all in my face that I was yearning for him, but he just shook his head.

"Not right now," he told me. "Maybe when I get back. I gotta meet up with my brothers.

Nodding my head, I sighed deeply as he walked away to the room to get himself ready to leave. By the time I turned back to my book, I couldn't even read it because my mind was so full of all the things he'd said.

There were so many layers to him and sometimes I felt like he'd never let me get below the surface. After hearing the little bit of his story that I did, I wasn't quite sure I really wanted to.

MALIAH

"It's thick in this bitch," Chynah exclaimed with excitement as we both looked around the club.

It was definitely swole. I didn't know what the hell was going on, but every nigga with money seemed to be in the club that night and they weren't afraid to throw it either. I licked my lips as I looked at the crowd. All I saw was green and it was already getting me hype as hell.

"Aye, you next, Cali," Tony told me as he crept up behind me. "As you can see we got a good crowd here so you need to give these niggas a show."

Nodding my head, a small smile rose up on my face as I walked backstage to change into just the outfit that I needed to make sure that I stole the show. Never in life had I thought that this would be my life…stripping for money. But I had found a way to own this shit and I loved it.

I was tired of being a weak bitch who depended on a man to do every single thing for me. I did that with Danny and where did it get me? Broke, with three kids and living in the damn projects with not a dollar to my name.

There was something powerful about being able to get on stage and make niggas go crazy enough to spend all their money. I could do it like Beyoncé, just with less clothes on, and I was getting paid big time to do it, just like she did.

"NOW WE ABOUT TO BRING OUT ONE OF THE FINEST BITCHES YOU'VE EVER SEEN! Hailing from the West Coast, get ready to drop them hunnids for muthafuckin'

CALI MALI!" the announcer yelled when it was time for me to do my set.

The crowd roared and it was the drug I needed to get into my zone. Walking out on the stage like I owned it, I easily commanded the attention of every thirsty nigga in the club. The only man who didn't have his eyes on me was Jhonny, who Murk was paying to make sure that I was protected every night. And the only reason Jhonny didn't look was out of the respect he had for him.

A mix of "Nasty Girl" by Beyoncé with the slowed down bass line from "California Love" by Tupac came on and I started to sway my hips hypnotically before grabbing the pole and twerking on it. With a seductive smirk on my face, I teased the crowd by shimmying halfway out of my shorts.

"IF YOU WANNA SEE SOME PUSSY, DROP THAT MUTHAFUCKIN' GREEN! THIS BITCH AIN'T DOING THIS SHIT FOR FREE!"

Dollars began to fly as men tried their hardest to get me to the point where I would pull something off. I looked at all the money on the stage but I wasn't satisfied yet. I needed more.

Propping myself up on the pole, I untied my top and let the strings hang, but didn't allow it to fall. More money began to fly so I flipped upside down and let the top glide down to the stage, exposing my bountiful C-cup breasts. Then I spread my legs into a split and watched as the lust-eyed men began to salivate in anticipation of seeing the sweet pink between my thick thighs.

By the time I went upright, the stage was nearly covered with bills…most of them big faces. A satisfied smirk crossed my face. Now I could go ahead and give them what they wanted.

I'd just taken off all of my clothes and was in the middle of a forward split when I sensed the atmosphere in the club shift. Still dancing, I followed the heads of the other strippers scattered around the floor and saw them all staring at a group of men who had just walked into the club.

It was Legend, Murk, Quan and Dame. My teeth clenched but I tried to keep my cool. Murk and his brothers hadn't been to the club since the night they'd came in and caught me sucking dick in the private room. I figured they'd stayed away because Murk didn't want them there, but here they were.

Humiliated, I watched as Chynah's thirsty ass made her way right over to where they stood and grabbed Murk by the arm, which made my blood boil. He didn't even move to push her off when she leaned over to whisper in his ear. Trying to keep my mind on my dance and ignore the fuckery going on right in front of me, I continued to wind my hips. Even still, I couldn't help but keep my eyes on them as Chynah led them up to the V.I.P. section.

"Fuckin' bitch," I cursed under my breath.

Although we weren't official, most of the girls at the club knew that Murk and I messed around so it pissed me off that she would try me like that. Grinding my teeth together, I tried my best to finish my set so I could get the fuck off the stage and get the hell out of there. I had too much going on in my life to deal with this shit.

The crowd started to hoot even louder and I felt someone else's presence behind me. It was Candie, one of the few girls I was cool with. She started to dance alongside me and the money continued to pour in.

"Don't be bothered about that bitch," Candie said as we danced together. "Her ass is thirsty but Murk ain't stupid. I'm sure he sees her for the gold-diggin' hoe she is."

Flicking my eyes back over to the V.I.P., I looked at him and nodded my head. In light of everything going on between us, I wasn't quite sure but I hoped Candie was right.

Chapter Eleven

LEGEND

"Shawty done got thick, Murk," Quan snickered once we'd sat down in the V.I.P. section of the club.

"Nigga, shut the fuck up and stop looking at her stupid ass!" Murk spat back, jabbing him hard in the ribs.

Laughing, Quan doubled over, grabbing his side. Still furious, Murk sat back in his seat with his arms folded and a childish ass pout on his face as Maliah walked off the stage. I couldn't help but laugh at his ass.

"Murk, why da fuck you ask to come here if you got issues with niggas lookin' at your chick? Her ass is a dancer at the club!" I told him as I rolled up a blunt. "You buggin', nigga."

"She ain't my fuckin' chick," he grumbled as he sat up in his seat.

Me, Quan and Dame each exchanged identical looks. Whatever was going on with his ass was foreign to me, but he needed to get his shit together. If ever I move a bitch into my shit, she's mine. Especially if she got three mouths walking in behind her. But what he was doing wasn't my business so I grabbed my phone and sent a text to Shanecia. She was at the hospital visiting her sister, but I still wasn't cool with her being out and about by herself. However, I was learning that sometimes it didn't matter what I thought when it came to her hardheaded ass.

"Nigga, how you move a bitch and all three of her youngins into your spot and you sayin' she ain't yours? That's your woman, you just don't know that shit yet," Quan joked, saying the same thing that all of us were thinking.

"Naw, see, it's like this," Murk explained sitting up. "I care for her and shit…plus, I'm somewhat responsible for what happened to her baby daddy so I'mma look out for her ass, but I be damned if I fuck with a bitch on that level who is out showing her pussy to every nigga in the damn city."

"Ohhhh, so that's what your issue is," Dame chimed in, finally pulling his eyes away from one of the strippers long enough to respond. "You was trying to turn a hoe into a housewife and now you pissed because she still out here trying to be a hoe."

I raised one brow at Dame when he said that and looked at Murk waiting for him to knock him in his shit, but Murk didn't do a muthafuckin' thing. Grunting, I turned back to my phone. If it had been Shanecia he was talking about, I would've faded Dame's ass real quick.

"That's right," Murk agreed, pulling a half-smoked blunt from his pocket. He lit it and then took a pull.

"I told her that in order to be mine she had to leave this shit alone but she won't do it. It pisses me off because I keep gettin' mad about the shit but *she won't do it!* You know how chicks be talking that silly shit…" Murk shook his head and let his voice trail off.

"Yeah, I know what you mean," Quan inserted and then pulled his arms together, giving his best impression of a female. "'I just wanna have my *own* money and do my *own* thing! I don't wanna live off *yoooouuu*. I wanna be my *own* woman!' They say all that shit but let a nigga lose they muthafuckin' job and see if they don't drop his ass talkin' about 'I love Jim Bean but he can't provide so biiiiitch, I gotta move on and find me a *paid* nigga!'"

"That's what the fuck I'm talkin' 'bout," Murk said nodding his head. "She had a nigga who ain't do shit and she was willing to lay around and have babies for his bitch ass. And here I go taking care of shit but all she wanna do is pussy pop in the fuckin' club. Look how these niggas out here treatin' her ass! I'd be knockin' niggas off every fuckin' day messin' with her ass!"

Nodding my head, I started scrolling through my phone as I finished rolling my blunt. I saw his point. The D-Boys couldn't be caught fuckin' with a bitch that was willing to show her shit or twerk on some dick for any nigga with money. We had the respect of the hood and had to keep it that way. We were willing to die for our women and if we were going to take that risk, we had to have that same loyalty returned.

"Well, you not the most vocal nigga when it comes to talkin' 'bout your feelings and shit. Maybe if you just tell her how you feel about her instead of sleepin' on my muthafuckin' couch every night just so you can get her ass mad, she might quit!" Dame laughed before continuing. "At least when Trell think I'm out fuckin' with other chicks, I'm *really* out fuckin' other chicks. You got her ass thinkin' that you doing shit but you really at my crib eating Cheetos and watching Netflix and wearing the pajamas with the feet in them."

"Yo' jokin' ass done or is you finished?" Murk shot back, hitting Dame with a strong glare.

As much as I was getting a kick out of hearing them all go back and forth, I had to cut them off in a little bit but I was waiting for Alpha to show up first.

"Nigga, what you readin'?" Dame asked, peering over my shoulder. I was so engrossed in my phone that I hadn't realized he was behind me.

"None of yo' damn business!" I frowned as I locked my phone and placed it in my pocket.

"You was readin' a book…I saw the title. *'Beloved'*…" he announced to everyone. "Sounds like some rich white lady shit. Da fuck is that?"

"I heard of that!" Quan piped up. "It's that movie with Oprah Winfrey in it lookin' like a slave."

"Nigga, *every* movie she in she be lookin' like a damn slave. Wasn't she in Roots knockin' out old ass white chicks?" Murk asked.

"That was *The Color Purple*, fool," I corrected him. All of my brothers looked at me like I'd lost my mind.

"My lady is educated! She be puttin' me up on all that smart shit," I explained to them.

"That's why you readin' that *Beloved* shit?" Dame teased with a smile.

Annoyed, I ignored his ass. Just because he wanted to be ignorant his whole life didn't mean that I wanted to. Plus, I hated to feel like somebody knew some shit that I didn't know, so if Shanecia was gonna keep talkin' about that damn book, I was gonna read that shit. It wasn't half bad. The only crazy thing was it was making me remember some shit about my own past I wanted to forget.

"Enough of this kee-keeing and shit. Let's discuss business," I started as I lit my blunt.

Just like that, all of my brothers shook off the games and moved their chairs to crowd around me.

"I spoke to Alpha today. He's out handling something for me but he'll be here in a minute," I informed everyone before checking my watch. "We been attacking Mello's team every day busting on niggas and still ain't nobody giving up this nigga's location, or giving us any information worth shit. So I'm ready to start grabbing up their bitches so we can deliver a stronger message."

I sat back and took a pull from my blunt as I examined each of their faces. Though attentive, Murk wasn't moved one way or the other, Dame look surprised and Quan seemed to be uncomfortable as hell about the situation.

"Aye, you good?" I asked him, unable to hide the fact that I could see he had something on his mind.

"You sayin' you want to start popping on these nigga's fams now, bro?" he questioned me with his eyes narrowed. When I didn't react to his question, he turned to Dame.

"We can't mess with the family. Dame…tell this nigga, man."

"Tell him what?" Dame asked with a frown. "You forgetting that Mello grabbed up Neesy, drugged her ass and then pushed her out of the fuckin' car onto the side of the damn street? If we hadn't pulled up on him, he would've killed her just to get at us. You really think Legend give a fuck about any of those niggas' bitches?"

"Yo, what I wanna know is why yo' ass so fuckin' concerned about that nigga and his team of fuck boys," Murk piped up all of a sudden, looking directly into Quan's eyes. "Get your mind right, nigga."

Without blinking, I watched the expression change on Quan's face. Secretly, I had been wondering the same thing. Not only had his ass been asking me a lot of questions as of late, but now he was speaking to me about having pity on some random nigga's bitch. Ain't nobody have pity on *my* bitch!

"Don't make it seem like that, Murk. Y'all niggas are fam and you know I'll never go against my blood. I just don't know if I'm good with dragging innocent females into this shit."

"They not innocent," I spoke up finally. "Any bitch messing with a muthafucka in this game knows that she can get it just like he can get it. Neesy included. As far as I'm concerned and as far as you *should* be concerned, them bitches just as guilty as their niggas. They wouldn't hesitate to bust on your stupid ass if it meant protecting their nigga. Wanna know how I know? Because any female I'm fuckin' with better be ready to bust on a nigga to save my ass, if it ever comes to that shit!"

Right when I said that, Alpha walked up into the V.I.P section, startling Dame in the process. Dame nearly jumped five feet in the air before grabbing for his gun.

"Nigga, what you jumpin' for? You need to get the bitch out yo' heart," Alpha told him, laughing before reaching out to give him dap.

"Ain't no bitch in me," Dame replied, returning the dap. "I just wanted to make sure you wasn't Trell creeping up here to fade on a nigga."

Tossing back his head, Alpha laughed again and then greeted Murk and Quan.

"Drop a baby in her and I promise it will calm her ass down," Alpha replied before reaching out to grab the blunt from Quan.

"Ain't nothin' gone calm her ass down," Dame replied somberly.

Alpha walked over to give me dap but I didn't move to return it. I was ready to get right to the issue at hand.

"You did what I told you?" I asked him when he sat down.

"I did," he responded, holding out a piece of paper for me. "The weapons team should be delivering everything you asked for tomorrow morning. Here is the list of everything you gettin'. What you planning on doin' with all that ammo and shit? You asked for enough to start a fuckin' army, Legend."

I didn't answer. It wasn't none of his business until I told him it was. Eyeing the paper, I scanned it before tucking it in my pocket.

"Why the fuck they can't deliver until the morning? I thought I said I needed my shit tonight," I told him in an icy tone.

The blunt in his mouth dropped, pointing to the floor, as a somewhat panicked look crossed his face. My brothers all leaned in donning curious expressions as they looked from me to Alpha.

Unable to hide the tension in his face, Alpha started to laugh nervously before he pulled the blunt from his lips to answer.

"You serious?" he asked me with both his eyebrows in the air.

I didn't flinch. Looking from Quan to Murk to Dame before looking back to me, Alpha started moving his hands in an animated fashion as he responded.

"You know how much shit you asked for? They need time to get all that together. It ain't like you asked for simple shit!" he exclaimed.

Narrowing my eyes, I looked square into his. "What you mean 'they need time'? We the only ones they supplying, right? Why the hell would they ever run out? They never have in the past."

Helpless, Alpha looked back around at my brothers for a lifeline, but neither one of them were willing to help his ass.

"Of course…these my niggas and you know they only work for the D-Boys."

"What about the other shit that I just sent you to do? Did you do that?" I gritted, absentmindedly moving my hand so that it grazed my weapon. Alpha caught the movement but he didn't respond.

I felt myself getting pissed off the more that I eyed him. The look on his face let me know that he'd failed me with my other request, also. Earlier in the day, I'd gotten a name on a salon where a chick married to one of Mello's niggas worked at. I'd told Alpha to check it out for me and if she was there, I'd ordered him to grab her ass, tie her up and meet us at the club.

It was the reason that I needed the guns because I was planning on getting enough info out of her ass to move on some niggas immediately. Now I had no guns and no bitch.

"S—she wasn't at work today but I mean, I can try again tomorrow. I can't help that the bitch wasn't there!" he explained. Beside me, Murk clicked his teeth and shook his head with a grim look on his face.

Staring Alpha down with a piercing glare, I didn't respond right away. One thing I'd learned is to always trust my instincts and something wasn't sitting right with me when it came to Alpha right then. When I'd told him how important it was for me to have the weapons delivered that night, he assured me it could be done and even checked with the dealer to ensure that they could do it.

Not only that, but the same informant who told me about the salon also told me that the chick had been there. I was more furious with myself than anything because if I hadn't been fucking around with Shanecia, I would have moved on the info my damn self. But if I had to do every fuckin' thing, what the hell I got a team for?

Now here he was telling me that the shipment wouldn't come until the next morning and that he hadn't grabbed up the chick. But the way that he was acting all nonchalant about it was what was getting to me. Everybody knew that I nutted the fuck up when shit didn't go the way that I laid out for it to go. For that reason, niggas told me shit ahead of time if there was a glitch in the plan. But here this nigga was telling me he fucked up and was acting all unapologetic about the shit.

Bowing his head, Alpha shrunk out of my glare, averted his eyes and then grabbed his phone before beginning to thumb through it. And that's when I fuckin' lost it.

Slapping the phone out of his hand, I waited for it to fall to the ground and stomped the shit out of it until the screen was completely cracked into little pieces.

"You wait until it's GO time to tell me that you fucked up?!" I yelled.

I was loud but not louder than the speakers, so everything in the strip club continued on as normal behind us. No one below us even knew that Alpha was about a second away from getting the shit knocked out of him.

"Legend, man, calm down! It's no biggie, I just—"

"No biggie?!"

With supernatural speed, I pulled my gun out and held it at my side. Murk stood up quietly, as always, ready to go if I said the word. Quan looked shocked about the entire altercation, but it was Dame who stood up to be the voice of reason.

"Aye, Legend. This is Alpha…cut this nigga some slack, yo!" Dame pled as Alpha sat quietly with a devastated look on his face.

"Who the fuck cuts slack?" Murk questioned while narrowing his eyes at Alpha.

"Legend…Don't do this shit! H—he's like a brother to us," Quan piped in. I cut him a look of disbelief as I continued to grip the banger at my side.

"Yeah but he's *not* a brother to us," I reminded him. "And you of all people, Quan, should know that blood don't mean shit sometimes. Or should I remind you about Quentin?"

The mere mention of that name silenced both Quan and Dame. With my point proven, I turned my attention back to Alpha as they backed down to allow me to continue.

"Truth is, nigga, you been missing a lot of meetings and shit. That day Neesy got snatched, you were supposed to be with us at Mello's crib, but you missed out on that too."

I paused for a second as I thought about my statement.

"Matter of fact, where the fuck *were* you?" I asked suddenly.

That day I'd been so preoccupied with the fact that I'd nearly killed Shanecia's sister and then finding out that Mello had grabbed her, that I'd never thought about how Alpha was supposed to have been with us but didn't show up.

"I—I had to handle some business with Omega and then I ran

late collectin' on some niggas moving weight for us on the Southside. By the time I got to the meet up spot, y'all was gone and..." his voice trailed off because he knew he'd fucked up yet again. There was no excuse he could have come up with that would have mattered to me.

My jaw clenched as I began to get more and more furious. Closing my eyes, I tried to count to a hundred really quick so that I could calm myself down. After killing Sinai, the only nigga we had on our team that we could trust other than each other was Alpha. I had to calm myself down so I could think straight before I blew this nigga's brains out.

"Get lost, niggaaaa," Murk warned him with his deep baritone, his words drawn out as if he were singing. Reaching out, he gave Alpha a hard nudge towards the exit.

Relieved, Alpha didn't hesitate for a second. Jumping up out of his seat, he scampered out of V.I.P. so fast that he was down the stairs and out the door before I was even able to count to twenty in my mind.

"Quan, get the car ready to ride out," I ordered suddenly. "We riding out tonight and fuckin' some shit up regardless. That nigga ain't stopping shit."

Nodding his head, Quan jumped up to do as I asked. Dame let out a protracted sigh and then grabbed his phone out of his pocket.

"Let me call Trell and let her know I might not be coming home tonight because Legend is on one," he muttered before getting up to walk out.

Clenching my jaw, I anxiously ran my hand over my face. I was stressed the fuck out. When I opened my eyes, Murk was looking me dead in the face.

"What's goin' on with you, bro?" he asked. "I can tell somethin' fuckin' with you."

Shaking my head, I wondered if I should tell Murk what was on my mind. After thinking it over for a few seconds, I decided to go ahead and do it. Out of anyone in the world, including my other brothers, Murk was the only nigga that no one could ever tell me would betray me. If I ever found out that he was working against me, it would fuck my whole mind up. I knew I could trust him.

"Neesy told me that she heard a voice that she recognized," I explained to him with a sigh. "When she was in the car with Mello, she said that there was a nigga ducked down in the backseat and the voice seemed familiar to her. She was too fucked up to know who it was for sure, but she was certain she heard it until I questioned her on it."

Murk gave me a look. "You sure she wasn't imaginin' that shit? She ain't been around nobody but us!"

"Us and Alpha," I corrected him. "And no lie, Quan been on some bullshit lately, too. Questionin' my moves and shit...What the fuck is up with that nigga, man?"

Clicking his tongue against his teeth, Murk gave me a disapproving look. "Don't let this shit with Neesy get your head fucked up. Quan is not Quentin."

Pulling my lips into a straight line, I reluctantly nodded my head as I tried to believe in my heart that he was right.

"Listen, I don't mean no disrespect but...Neesy was high as fuck. Her ass ain't know the sky from the crack of her ass when we got to her. Stop thinkin' so hard on that shit and let's get these niggas. Stop fuckin' with your team before you ain't got no team," Murk told me finally.

Looking at him, I nodded my head once more before grabbing him and pulling him into a half hug.

"I'll meet you back at the whip. You go over there and kiss yo' girl good night. Let her know you won't be back until the morning but it's because you're with me and not because you're hidin' at Dame's house," I said with a light chuckle when Murk frowned at me.

"I ain't tellin' her ass shit! Long as she shakin' her ass for dollar bills, she ain't got the right to tell me what the fuck to do!" he fumed before storming out ahead of me.

"Ole poutin' ass nigga," I said under my breath.

Shaking my head, I laughed and started to walk out the V.I.P. section. The entire way out the club, Murk kept his eyes on Maliah as she sauntered around the floor half-dressed. One look at his face let anyone know he was mad as hell and about two seconds from clicking on any nigga who paid her the least bit of attention.

It was as obvious as a monkey sitting in the middle of a pool of fish to anyone who may have been watching. Murk had it bad for Maliah and his stubborn ass didn't even know it.

Chapter Twelve

SHANECIA

"No change at all?" I asked Darin as I walked into Tanecia's room.

He looked like shit. His already overgrown beard was uneven and matted; the other hair on his face was growing in making him have a disheveled, messy and unkempt look. His clothes were wrinkled and he was so tired that worry lines were deeply etched into his face.

"No, not really," he replied, shaking his head.

He pulled his attention away from Tanecia only to briefly look me in the face before turning back to her and grabbing her hand. The love that was in his eyes almost brought tears to mine. He truly loved my sister and this situation proved it.

"I've been trying to get in touch with mama but...she wasn't home when I stopped by," I told him with a sigh as I sat down in the chair next to him. "I know she's been at the house because it's a mess, and there was a half-eaten Popeyes' meal on the table last I went over there. I can only sneak over there when Legend's gone because if he knew I was there, he would beat my—"

I stopped short when I saw Darin tense up. Discussing my involvement with Legend was obviously still a sore spot for him.

"She had a baby," Darin said quietly. "She was pregnant."

My mouth dropped open and tears came to my eyes before I'd even realized it. It wasn't until my vision was completely blurred that I blinked them away and cleared my throat so I could speak.

"She was pregnant? Wh—why didn't you tell me that?"

"I only found out yesterday. The nurse assumed it was mine because I've been here every day with her. She came to tell me she was sorry about the loss..."

Darin's voice cracked. He cleared his throat and then looked at me.

"What really fucks with me is that she didn't feel like she could tell me any of this. If she was pregnant from that nigga and she felt like she had to deal with him just because he was the father of her baby... why wouldn't she just tell me that?"

I didn't answer him because there was no answer I could give him to erase the pain he was feeling.

"Why don't you go home for a little bit? I'll stay here...just go shower and rest up. Come back in the morning," I advised, hoping he would listen.

Surprisingly, he exhaled heavily and nodded his head.

"I guess I'll give you some time alone with her," he replied. Then a small, weak smile crossed his face.

"I guess I could at least go wash my ass."

Cutting my eyes at him, I smirked and nodded my head agreement.

"Yeah, those lil' bird baths you been taking in the sink can't do the job forever. I'll stay with her until you come back in the morning."

"Okay," Darin responded.

Standing up, he leaned down and gave me a half hug then took one last look at Tanecia before walking out the room. Once he'd left, I texted Legend to let him know that I would be staying at the hospital with Tanecia and then placed my phone down on the table and fell asleep.

A few hours later, I woke up with a dry mouth and a crook in my neck. After checking Tanecia, my first thought was to check my phone but there was nothing from Legend. I couldn't ignore the feeling of dread that swelled up in my chest. It wasn't like him not to reply to my messages.

Standing up, I yawned loudly and then walked out in the hall to the elevator so I could go down to the third floor and get something to drink. When I walked out, I saw a familiar face sitting in a chair across from the room. It was Brandon. Legend had apparently gotten my message and sent him to watch over me.

"Where you goin'?" he inquired as I walked by him.

"I'm just gettin' something to drink."

He started to get up and I put my hands up to stop him.

"You don't have to trail me. I just need a minute to myself and I'll be right back. It's right down the hall."

Uncertain as to whether he should listen or not, Brandon gave me a warning look.

"You got five minutes and I'm coming for you," he said. I nodded my response and scurried away before he could change his mind.

The hospital was quiet for the most part because it was late. Some members of the night crew were cleaning to get prepared for the next day, but everyone else was either watching TV or thumbing through their phones instead of working.

After grabbing a Coke from the soda machine, I pressed the button to the elevator and flipped through my phone as I waited for it to arrive. Other than a few messages from Maliah about how Murk wasn't shit, there wasn't anything there. I made a mental note to call her later to hear what she had to say about Murk, and then placed the phone in my pocket just as the elevator buzzed.

The doors opened and an older black man pushing a mop and bucket scooted by me, before I stepped inside and pressed the button to Tanecia's floor. Just as the door was about to close, he lost his balance and stumbled backwards, knocking over the bucket. The water fell onto the floor and I jumped back off the elevator.

"I'm sorry, ma'am!" the man told me once he steadied himself with my help. "I'll clean up this mess and then you'll be good to go."

Looking at my watch, I saw that I had about a minute left before Brandon would come looking for me. Anxiously, I watched as the older man slowly mopped at the water on the floor of the elevator. My eyes surveyed the area and I saw another elevator open up.

"I'm going to use the other one," I told him as I ran to catch it. "Thank you!"

I slid into the elevator just in time and mashed the button to close the doors so that I could hurry and return. When the doors open, I walked hurriedly towards Tanecia's room but stopped suddenly when I saw a woman pause in front of her door, check the name on the outside and then peer inside.

Squinting, I walked right up to the fair-skinned woman, so light in complexion that she almost looked white. She had dark sunglasses on her face, a nice designer dress and a scarf tied tightly around her neck. Her dark, wavy hair was pulled into a tight bun at the back of her head and as she stood in front of Tanecia's room, she was clutching what I recognized as a very expensive Birkin bag, only because Tanecia had the same one.

"Can I help you?" I asked her as I walked up to her side.

Checking the space where Brandon had been, I saw he'd left. He had been serious about those five minutes.

"No, I'm just visiting a friend," she replied and moved to walk into the room.

"Well, who are you and how do you know my sister?" I inquired further as I looked her up and down.

"Your sister?" she repeated. "Oh…" She started to laugh. "My mistake. The person I'm looking for doesn't have a sister. I must be at the wrong room. Silly me!"

Twisting up my lips, I glared at her, not quite believing the little act she was putting on. And I was just about to tell her that when a voice thundered out from behind me.

"There you are!" Brandon shouted before starting to wheeze.

Spinning around, I watched as he clomped towards me with his hand on his rattling chest. While panting profusely, he reached into his pocket and pulled out an inhaler, took a deep pull and then sighed in relief as his breathing became less labored.

This the kinda security Legend got for me? I thought as I watched Brandon.

"Don't get it twisted, Neesy. Legend trusts me with you because I'm a sure shot. Ain't a bullet I've ever released that didn't hit the target," he explained as if reading my thoughts. "This asthma just be fuckin' with me. I told your ass five minutes! Elevator out so a nigga had to use the stairs to try and track your ass…"

He continued talking but I suddenly remembered the suspicious acting woman who I was talking to, and turned around. She was gone.

"Brandon…did you see the lady that I was talking to?" I asked him. "Did you see where she went?"

"You mean that white lady? Yeah…she walked that way. Out the door," he pointed to the exit at the other end of the hall.

Stepping in that direction, I thought about following her but I figured there was no use. By now, if she was trying to get away, she was long gone.

"That's right," Brandon wheezed as he sat down and tried to collect himself by taking another puff of his inhaler. "Stay your ass where the hell I can see you. Don't your ass get any funny ideas. A nigga almost died just now running behind your ass."

Shaking my head at him, I took one more look down the hall and then walked inside of Tanecia's room. Stepping past the window to get to my chair, I looked out and saw a cream big-body Bentley tearing out of the parking lot, and my instincts told me that I could probably guess who it was inside.

I tore my eyes away from the car and back to Tanecia's unconscious frame. What other enemies did she have?

Chapter Thirteen

MALIAH

"So wait...what?" I asked Shanecia as I soaked my feet in some Epsom salt.

The night before I'd worn some high heels that were cute as hell but killed my damn feet. When I woke up that morning, I had corns popping out every damn where. Being that I was too sexy to be sporting some 'paul bunions', I immediately started soaking them so I could get it together before I had to get ready to hit the club again.

I was working nearly every night, but that would soon change. The way I was raking in money, I would soon be able to scale back to only four days a week instead of six.

"I caught some white lady trying to sneak into Tan's room. Before I could really get in her ass, she got away, but I'm telling you that there was something shady about her," she said. "I feel like Mello sent her."

Laughing, I rolled my eyes. "Neesy, since when street niggas started using little prissy white ladies to do their dirty work? You tripping."

"Maybe I am," she told me with a sigh. "But, either way, I convinced Legend and Darin to pay to convert a room in Darin's house for her to stay in. They are setting up the equipment now and she'll have an around the clock nursing staff to watch after her."

"You might be takin' this lost little white lady a bit too seriously," I mumbled. "But this the kinda shit folks do when they have money to blow."

"Huh?"

"Nothing," I replied back. My call-waiting beeped in my ear. "Hold on, Neesy. Never mind, just let me call you back." I clicked over before she could respond. "Hello?"

"Li-Li," Danny's sexy voice came through the line, instantly taking me down a lane of memories that I needed to forget.

"Yes, Danny?"

"I just wanted you to know that I'm still not using. It's been weeks and…I'm not gone lie…I've had urges but I haven't done anything."

Rolling my eyes, I scoffed at him. "That's because you don't have any money, Danny. As soon as you get some, you just gone go and—"

"I *do* have money! I told you about my cousin with the mechanic shop in Pembroke Pines! I've been working *and* saving my money. I almost got enough to move into a place."

Now that was a surprise. When we were together, Danny hadn't been able to save five dollars once he'd started using. To hear that he'd been working and was able to save up enough for a place, was shocking to me to say the least.

"I just want to see my kids, Maliah. I don't want them thinkin' their daddy is dead!"

"They don't think you're dead," I finally confessed to him with a sigh. "I never had that talk with them. I simply told them that you were away."

Danny didn't say anything for a while and I heard a noise that sounded like a stifled sob.

"Are you okay?"

"Yeah, I'm good," he said, trying to maintain his normal tone, but his voice cracked and gave him away. He sniffled and it pained me to know that he was so distraught that he was actually shedding tears. He really did miss his family.

"Can I just talk to them? Or hear their voice? You don't have to tell them it's me…I just want to hear my babies."

That broke me. One thing about Danny was that, when he was well, he was a wonderful father and I knew he loved his kids. But addiction was a strong disease and once it got a hold of him, he couldn't see anything else. However, in my heart of hearts, I knew there wasn't anyone he loved more than the kids.

"Don't say anything," I told him.

"I won't."

I battled myself mentally for a moment before saying 'what the hell' and going ahead with it.

"Shadaej!" I called out.

Seconds later, she came running from her room with two hands wrapped around the brand new Barbies that Murk had bought for her. LeDejah came out right behind her with open markers in her hand, and DeJarion followed with his face nearly covered with all kinds of drawings of all colors, courtesy of the artist, LeDejah.

"Give me that!" I said snatching the markers from LeDejah's hands. "Dej, why would you color on your brother's face?"

LeDejah's head dropped shamefully. "I'm sorry, mama."

"We wanted to give him tattoos on his face like Mu—"

"Don't draw on Jari's face! Okay, Dej?" I asked, cutting Shadaej off before she mentioned Murk's name.

"Okay!"

"Tattoos on his face like who, Sha?" Danny's voice erupted from the phone. I didn't even have him on speakerphone but he was loud enough for all of us to hear him.

"DADDYYYYY!" Shadaej and LeDejah chorused as DeJarion clapped along happily.

"I told you not to talk!" I yelled into the phone at Danny, placing the phone to my ear.

"Li-Li, tell me you don't have my kids around another nigga?" he asked me in a way that made me feel guilty for some reason. "Don't tell me that you won't let me be around my kids but you'll let another nigga."

"Danny, ain't no nigga around your kids!" I lied. "And I don't appreciate you doing what you just did. You know what? I'mma call you later."

And with that I hung up the phone. When I looked up, all of my kids were looking right into my eyes. DeJarion didn't seem to be bothered at all, but Shadaej and LeDejah both had tears in their eyes.

"Why didn't you let me speak to my daddy?" Shadaej asked me. "I missed him. Why can't I speak to him?"

"Did daddy do something bad?" LeDejah asked me. Of all three of my babies, she was the thinker. She was always trying to make sense of things and figure everyone out.

"Daddy didn't do anything bad. He just has to fix a few things. But in order for him to fix them so he can see you, you both have to promise me something," I told them. My heart panged with guilt for what I was about to do.

"What, mommy?" Shadaej asked, wiping at her moist eyes.

"You have to keep daddy a secret for now. You can't tell anyone that you spoke to daddy because then he won't be able to finish what he needs to do, okay?"

With wide eyes, Shadaej nodded her head in agreement. Not as convinced, LeDejah gave me a skeptical look but then eventually nodded her head, although it was obvious she wasn't buying my explanation.

"Okay, y'all go play before I have to take you to Grandma's," I told them as I glanced at my watch. "And don't be drawing on Jari's face!"

They ran gleefully down the hallway back to the room as I sat, still soaking my feet in Epsom salt and crumbling under the weight of my guilt.

***

"Shit! I'm running late!" I groaned as I ran around the house looking for some shimmering cream I'd bought earlier in the day.

I loved the way that it made my skin glow under the stage lights. Being that I was slightly superstitious, I also believed it was necessary since the first time I'd worn it I brought in more money than I'd ever earned before.

"Got it!"

Leaning over the couch, I grabbed it just as the front door opened and Murk walked into the room.

"Daaaamn! Pull over, that ass too fat," he joked as he walked over and smacked me on my backside that was still positioned in the air. With the lotion in my hand, I pushed his hand away as I tried to stand upright.

"You got jokes, huh?" I asked then poked out my mouth as I looked at him.

He looked sexy in his all-blue outfit with matching suede blue J's, but I wasn't going to tell his ass that. Murk was cocky and arrogant enough without me blowing up his big ass head.

"Remember that vacation we went on with Legend and yo' cousin?" he asked me as he opened the fridge and grabbed a Heineken.

"Yeah, you mean the one where I didn't get to see shit because you wanted to fuck the whole time?"

Popping open the top, he grinned. "Yeah, that one. Wanna go on another one? With the kids?"

He peered at me over the top of the bottle and waited for me to respond. Something about the way he was looking at me made me get the eerie feeling that I was being tested. It felt like he'd been doing that a lot lately.

"So you're cool with going on vacation with the kids?"

Placing the bottle firmly onto the table next to him, he nodded his head and frowned.

"Why wouldn't I be cool with that?"

Biting my lip, I didn't answer him. He stood up and walked over to me and then laced his arms around my waist, pulling me close.

"I'm not like these other niggas, Li," he told me as he looked into my eyes. "Do I act like them other niggas?"

He waited for me to reply and I shook my head 'no'. Murk was a lot of things, but one thing he wasn't was like anyone else I'd ever met.

Leaning forward with his hips, he pushed until I could feel his hard erection poking me firmly against the thigh.

"Do I *feel* like these other niggas?" he asked haughtily.

"Hell naw," I cooed.

"You sure?" he questioned with a smirk.

Before I could answer, he brought his hand forward and slipped his fingers through the band of my tights, pushing further down until he was running two fingers over my clit.

"I'm s-s-s-sure," I stuttered as my knees began to get weak.

"Where the kids at?" he asked me.

"Who?" I replied, totally forgetting everything else around me.

"The kids, nigga!" he repeated, pulling his hand from my pants and breaking my hypnotic state.

"Oh! In the room…sleeping. I was about to wake them up so I could take them over to—"

"Shhhhh," Murk shushed me as he started to peel down my tights.

Once they were down to my knees, he pulled my legs apart, lifted me up and swung around, pinning me between his body and the wall. Reaching down, he released his thick, bulging anaconda from his jeans and I licked my lips in anticipation.

"Let me suck it…"

"We ain't got all that time," Murk told me as he ran his thumb over the head and prepared to push in. "I gotta get you right real quick and then we'll finish off in the room so we don't get caught."

I giggled at him saying 'get caught' as if we were two teenagers trying to have sex quietly in the house before my parents walked in and caught us. Shushing me once more, Murk leaned back and pushed his girth into me, instantly making my giggles turn to quiet moans as he eased in and out of me. He held me up with a hand supporting each thigh as he slammed into me, pushing my back hard against the wall.

Suddenly, he moved his hands up and spread my cheeks apart. When he started running his finger across my ass as he pushed harder and harder into me, I lost my mind. Within seconds, I creamed all over his rod as I blubbered incoherent words in languages I didn't even know I knew.

"You like that nasty shit, huh?" he smiled as he released me onto my feet.

He smacked me hard on my ass and pointed to the room. Happy to oblige, I kicked my tights the rest of the way off and took off down the hall so I could get some more. I knew I was late as hell for work, but it was the furthest thing from my mind.

"Face down, ass up," he demanded as soon as he walked in behind me and closed the door.

Poking out my bottom lip, I hesitated for a minute before moving to follow his request, but he caught it.

"Something wrong?" he asked.

His hazel eyes were filled with concern but mine began to fill up with lust as I watched him standing in front of me stroking his thick, erect pole, still glistening from my juices.

"It's just…we're always *fuckin'*," I told him.

"What?" He frowned and dropped his hands by his side. "The hell you complainin' about? You love this dick!"

"That's not what I mean, Murk." I paused as I tried to think of a way to explain to the least emotional man in the world that I wanted him to be a little more sensitive with me.

"I mean…I want to cuddle, hug, kiss and stuff. Like, we can do it slow sometimes before we go fast—"

"Maliah, this starting to sound like you on some soft shit," he mumbled and I could see his erection going down. I was losing him.

"Like…you ain't never made love before?" I asked finally. He didn't answer and the blank look on his face was hard to read.

"Okay, just lay down. Let me show you," I told him with a sigh.

"Hell naw. I ain't laying down and you ain't showing me shit. You sound like you wanna pinch a nigga's nipples. I ain't with that gay shit, Li."

Reaching down, he grabbed his dick in his hands and squeezed hard as he continued to talk.

"You see this? This shit ain't for decoration! I tote this muthafucka around because I beats the pussy up, ya feel me? You ain't bout to be in here lickin' circles around my belly button or some shit. Da fuck you think this is?"

Ignoring his 'alpha male' rant, I walked over and got right in front of him and then dropped to my knees. Opening my mouth wide, I deep-throated him, sucking him down my throat until he was almost standing on his toes.

"Gooooooot damn!" he groaned. "Fuck, you ain't never done this shit before!"

I continued to suck harder and harder, using my tongue to spell words on his mushroom head until he finally grabbed the back of my head and released a milky, thick stream of hot cum right down my throat. Pulling away, I swallowed it all down and wiped the corners of my mouth as he looked at me intensely with astonishment.

"Go sit on the bed," he told me, still staring into my eyes. "I wanna hear more about this love shit you said you want me to do to you."

Laughing, I stood up and shook my head. "So I just gotta give you some good head to make you listen?"

"Hell yeah!"

"Murk, you are a mess," I told him as I walked into the adjoining bathroom to freshen up so I could drop the kids off and go to work.

"What you doin'?" he asked, popping the door open right as I grabbed my toothbrush and toothpaste.

"What you think? I gotta go to work!"

As soon as I mentioned work, Murk's mood shifted and it became clear to me what his problem was. I was starting to notice that we never had issues until work came up. How I'd missed it all this time, I didn't know, but now it was clear.

"Li-Li, I don't want you workin' at the club no more," Murk told me authoritatively. He pointed back into the room. "Now, Li, get your ass back in the bed so we can fuck and make love."

I rolled my eyes at his disrespectful ass.

"Murk, we've talked about this before. I'm not quitting the club… I'm making my own money. I appreciate everything you've done for me as far as the house and the car, but I want to have my own shit! I don't want to be posted up in your place forever!"

Glaring at me, Murk folded his arms in front of his chest. After waiting for me to get my mind right, he lifted his hand up and grabbed at his chin while he spoke.

"So what you trying to tell me is that your plan is to stay here until you get your money right and then move?"

Blinking a few times, I repeated what he said in my head and then nodded. "Yes, that's exactly my plan."

Murk clenched his jaw before responding.

"Well, the good thing about having a plan A is that there is always a muthafuckin' plan B when you find out you was planning on doing some dumb shit! So you can dead your little bright idea because you ain't goin' nowhere!"

"You can't tell me what to do! You aren't my man, remember?! Your ass is always reminding me of that shit so don't try to pull rank now," I shot back. I was starting to get irritated as hell of going back and forth with him about the same thing.

"Da fuck?! I *am* your man! But you ain't my woman until you stop shaking your ass at the damn club!"

Confused as hell, I screwed my face up and squinted at him. "You're my man but I'm not your woman? Nigga, that don't even make no damn sense!"

"No, what don't make no sense is that you got a good nigga right here that's willing to take care of you and all twelve of your kids but you won't stay your ass off the fuckin' pole!"

He grabbed both of my arms and squeezed so tight that I tried to wiggle away.

"Don't you know how many women would love to be with a nigga who loved them enough to tell them *not* to work? How many niggas you know walkin' around tellin' chicks to stop workin'...to sit back and let their man take care of everything?"

I heard every single thing that Murk said, but my mind was stuck on what he said right at the beginning.

"'A nigga who loved them enough to tell them not to work'? You trying to tell me you love me?"

"What?" he questioned releasing my arms. "I didn't say that shit."

"Yes, you did!" I told him. "You *did* say that."

"Shut up."

"Okay fine, well I need to get ready for work," I baited him as I put toothpaste on my toothbrush.

"Do whatever the fuck you need to do," he muttered under his breath.

I brushed my teeth and washed up, the whole time counting out how many more nights I would have to work to get to the goal I'd set for myself of how much money I wanted in my savings account. Murk's words were in my head and I was slowly deciding to alter my plan and quit the club. I just needed to get my cake up first so if anything went wrong, I'd never find myself having to rely on another man again.

"Okay," I said as I walked out of the bathroom. Murk was lying on the bed with his feet crossed at the ankles and the remote in his hand, cruising through the channels.

"I'm going to get the kids in the car so I can take them to my mama's and I'll be out."

"You ain't takin' my shorties nowhere," he replied. "They sleepin' peacefully and that's how they gone stay."

Rolling my eyes, I threw on some clothes and got ready to leave. Murk had to feel like he was the victor over something, so I decided not to even argue about the kids. I'd let him have that.

Chapter Fourteen

SHANECIA

B*oom! Boom! Boom!*

The sound of someone banging on the door jerked me right out of sleep. Jumping to my feet, I ran over to the nightstand and grabbed the gun that Legend kept in there. He told me it was there when I first moved in and even gave me a run down on how to use a gun.

Listen, Neesy. One in the chamber, pull the trigger and shoot... I thought as I ran his instructions through my mind.

My heart was racing just as fast as my thoughts, as I tried to figure out whether to go to the door, call 9-1-1 or to call Legend.

Neesy, get a hold of yourself, I thought finally. *You don't even know who the hell is at the door!*

Taking a deep breath, I pursed my lips and straightened my shoulders as I walked to the door slowly. Legend wasn't home, as usual. To tell the truth, I was getting used to spending my nights alone. He was always out handling business and he never explained himself when he walked in early in the morning. I knew Legend was working and not messing around on me, but it didn't make it any easier.

Creeping to the door with the gun still tightly wrapped in my grasp, I leaned over and peered out the peephole while holding my breath so I wouldn't make a sound.

When I looked through to the other side, I saw a short, thick, light-skinned chick standing on the other side with a duffle bag in one hand and her other hand placed on her large, curvy hip. Her buttery complexioned seemed flushed red and her expression showed very clearly that she was pissed off to the max.

Frowning, I wondered to myself who this woman could be.

"Who is it?" I asked through the door, still clutching the gun. If it was one of Legend's old flames popping up, I might still have use for it in order to shoot her and shoot his ass too, for lying and telling me that he'd never brought chicks to his new place.

"Trell!" she yelled out in a heavy voice, instantly reminding me of Jennifer Hudson for some strange reason.

Walking to the kitchen, I placed the gun into one of the drawers before running to the front door and opening it.

"Thank you, sister girl," Trell said with a heavy exhale.

Without waiting for me to invite her in, she stormed past me, dragging her duffle bag behind her, then dropped it on the floor before rushing into the kitchen to pour herself a drink.

"Make yourself at home," I muttered as I closed the front door and locked it.

When I stepped into the kitchen, Trell had her head tossed back and was gulping down the last little bit of water from a water bottle she'd grabbed out the fridge. I walked over across from her and placed my elbows on the countertop, my chin in my hands and stared at her.

"Well, hello…I'm Neesy."

"I know," she replied breathlessly as she pulled the bottle from her lips. "And I'm sorry for being rude but I didn't have nowhere else to go, and I had to get the fuck out of my house before I committed murder!"

"Murder?" I asked with both of my eyebrows in the air.

"Yes!" she exclaimed with a frown. She eyed me as if she were trying to figure out whether or not I was hard of hearing or simply too touched in the head to comprehend what she was saying.

"Neesy, who is making all that noise—"

Maliah walked in looking like a zombie with her hair in a messy ponytail and still in the pajamas I'd loaned her, scaring the shit out of me. I'd forgotten that she was spending the night until that moment.

Maliah had come over, furious and banging on the front door around 3 in the morning, after going home and finding out that Murk had changed the locks on her ass. After calling him and pounding on the door, she'd decided just to sleep over at my place until the morning.

"This is Trell," I told her, holding my hand out towards Trell. "Trell, this is Li-Li, Murk's girlfriend. Li-Li, this is Trell, Dame's girlfriend."

"That nigga is *not* my man any more, Neesy, I swear!" Trell replied.

Immediately, she got teary-eyed which had me feeling all kinds of awkward. Making a fist with one hand, she pounded it into the other as she spoke.

"I'm so muthafuckin' tired of that nigga running games on me like I'm stupid! Look at me. I'm sexy as hell!"

She paused to give us a chance to look at her bodacious body. I couldn't even do anything but nod my head. Trell had it going on. She wasn't no skinny chick. She was thick…like Serena thick, with a tiny waist, large hips, thick thighs and a fat ass.

Everything a brother loved about a black woman, she had it. Her creamy, bronze complexion was smooth and glowed. The reddish, brown color of her hair was a perfect match up to give her a regal look, almost queenly. The way she dressed, perfectly flattered her shape and she had great taste. Whatever reason Dame had for cheating on her couldn't possibly have anything to do with looks, because she owned that department.

"There are a lot of men out here who wouldn't hesitate to have me and treat me right. Why I keep messing around with Dame's clown ass, I will never know! Now he keeps coming in whenever he wants to and his excuse is always the same: 'Legend got me doin' shit. I gotta be there for my fam.' Fuck all of them! I know they be lying to me when I ask them if Dame is fuckin' around on me!"

She burst out in tears and I turned to give Maliah a look, but she wasn't even looking in my direction. Maliah walked over to where Trell was standing and sat on the barstool across from her.

"Girl, I know exactly what you goin' through. Murk's ass does the same thing to me. He thinks he can come in all time of night too, like I'mma go for that shit," she told her as she reached over and patted Trell's hand sympathetically.

"But that's different," Trell said, grabbing a napkin from the counter to dab sorrowfully at her eyes. "Murk is acting like that with you because you out here acting like a hoe. My nigga really *is* a hoe!"

"WHAT?!" Maliah snapped, snatching her hand back from Trell's. "What you mean I'm actin' like a hoe? You don't know me like that!"

"Girl, don't act like you haven't realized Murk is acting an ass only because he wants you to stop stripping and you refuse. That man loves you and he ain't doin' shit but trying to piss you off. All them nights you think he's out with a bitch, he's been layin' up on my couch lookin' like a lost puppy and eatin' up all my damn food!"

Trell rolled her eyes as Maliah's rose to the ceiling while she thought on her words.

"That actually makes sense, Li-Li," I replied, sitting on the barstool next to her. "Murk isn't the type to really talk about his feelings so it makes sense that he would do some childish shit like that."

"But he didn't ask me to stop stripping until yesterday," Maliah said finally. "Not once did he ask me that before. He said if I was going to be his lady, I had to stop…once we were official. We aren't even official."

Blowing out a breath, Trell rolled her eyes once again. "If you don't know anything about the Dumas brothers, know this: they will say a little and expect you to just figure out the rest. Murk didn't ask you to stop stripping because he assumed if you wanted to be with him, you'd make the choice your own self. Murk and Legend don't like *asking* for *shit* and they won't."

Once again, she was right. I nodded my head and looked at Maliah. Just from noting the expression on her face, I could see that she knew Trell was right, too.

"Anyways, I caught an Uber over here to ask if I could borrow some money to catch a plane. I'm going back home. I'm sick of Dame and his shit. So…I'm leaving him," she said.

My lips parted slightly as I watched her to see if she was serious.

"You're leaving?" I asked to make sure I'd heard her correctly.

Although I hadn't met Trell, I'd heard enough about her relationship with Dame to know this was a big step for her. As much as Dame cheated on Trell, everyone knew he loved her. They'd been together for years and I was positive that it would fuck him up inside once he found out she was gone.

"Yes, I'm leaving. My parents live in Virginia so I'm going back home. I can't deal with Dame's shit anymore. I only packed a few things and I didn't take any of his money. So if you don't mind me borrowing a few dollars for a plane ticket, I promise I'll pay Legend back," she told me.

"Here you go, girl," Maliah chimed in. She leaned over the table behind us, grabbed her purse and pulled out a handful of bills before dropping them on the counter.

"I want to support the struggle because I been where you are before."

Scoffing, I cut my eyes at Maliah before turning to Trell.

"I'm more than happy to help you out and you don't have to pay me back. And damn…I'm sorry we met like this!"

"Chile, ain't nobody sorry except for Dame's sorry ass," Trell replied, rolling her eyes. "I'm sick of his shit. Last week, I woke up with something that, thankfully, I could go to the clinic and get rid of. It ain't even been a week later and he's already back at this shit again. Next time, I may not be so lucky."

Catching her drift, I nodded my head and handed her a few bills out of my purse.

"Do you need a ride to the airport?" I asked.

"No, I'll be fine," Trell told me as she turned towards the door, picking up her duffle bag on the way. Suddenly, she swiveled around and gave me and Maliah a serious look.

"Please…please don't tell any of them where I'm going," she pled. "I need time and I don't want Dame to be able to talk me out of this."

Looking at her, I felt immediately connected to her and responsible for helping her get the emotional healing she needed. I'd heard about the things that Dame did to her and, had it been Legend, I would be crushed.

I shook my head. "I won't."

"Hey," I called just as she was to the door. "Remember, it takes a real man to know that one woman is enough."

And with that, Trell nodded her head and shot me a thin smile, before walking out the door and closing it behind her. I turned to Maliah and gave her a look.

"Can you believe she's leaving him?" I asked with wide eyes.

Maliah shook her head. "Hell naw. That nigga's mind is going to be fucked up. He does his dirt but I can tell he really loves her."

A shadow passed through Maliah's eyes and I had a feeling she was thinking about Danny. When I saw her eyes begin to glisten with tears, I knew I was right.

"Sometimes the ones we love can do us the most damage if we stay with them. It's best to leave them alone before they cause the kind of damage that can't be fixed," I told her and prayed that she was catching my message.

Nodding her head, Maliah sniffed back her tears and bit her bottom lip before saying, "You're right. That shit hurts like hell but I know you're right."

Chapter Fifteen

MALIAH

Opening up the kids' suitcase, I counted all of the outfits inside for the second time to make sure that I wasn't missing anything. Once I was satisfied that they had everything they needed, I closed it back and sighed.

"How long y'all gonna be gone again?" I asked my mama when she waltzed into the room, her eyes searching to see if she was forgetting anything.

"Long as I feel like it! They aren't in school, Maliah. It should be fine for me to spend some time with my grandbabies!" she snapped at me.

"It is fine, mama. I just wanted to know when I should expect y'all to be back," I told her. "I'm just not used to them being away from me."

"I know, since you had pushed me out of your life," she reminded me hastily. "But now that I have the opportunity to bond with my grandbabies, I'd appreciate it if you stop worrying and carryin' on like I didn't raise you!"

Twisting up my lips, I scrutinized her as she grabbed a bottle of body spray and sprayed it liberally over her body.

"You sure you not goin' to meet up with no man?" I asked her with one brow lifted.

"Honey, *trust* if I was going to meet up with a man, I wouldn't be bringin' the kids along. It's been a long time since somebody done let me take a ride on top their Cadillac so, baby girl, if I ever get that chance again, best believe ain't gone be no time to be worried with no grandbabies! I'mma ride that thang until the wheels fall off!" she revealed to me as she wiggled her hips from side to side.

Fully disgusted at the thought of her riding someone's 'Cadillac', I turned my lips and nose up at her and focused my attention on Shadaej, LeDejah and DeJarion, who were sitting across from me watching TV and coloring. They weren't paying us the least bit of attention so I figured it was a good time to speak to her about Danny.

"Mama…remember when I told you about D?" I asked her. She nodded her head slowly and then walked over and sat next to me.

"He's been calling me. He got his life together and is about to move into his own place. He's workin' at his cousin's mechanic shop," I told her.

She cut her eyes at me. "I know what Daniel is up to, child."

"How…"

I started to ask but then caught myself. I didn't know how she did it but Ms. Berneice always managed to know somebody's business. She had to be the one sharing the news this time too.

"Don't get caught up with him again, Maliah," she warned me. "You're finally doing right by these kids. They look good, they are taken care of and you look damn good too. I don't know much about this Murk…What the hell is his name anyways?"

"Pablo," I said quietly.

"I don't know much about Pablo but I know that he doesn't say much, but he does a lot. In my experience, those are the men who wear their heart on their sleeve so you need to be careful."

She gave me a cautious look and I groaned. I was sick of everyone acting like I was some silly little girl. She patted my hand and then continued.

"A lot of men will scream 'I love you, I love you, I love you' until the cows come home, and have little silly girls all caught up in their empty words. The men who hesitate to say it right away…those are the ones who mean it. They are cautious because they know how powerful that statement is. He's not ashamed to admit it. He just knows a man in love has given a woman the power to destroy him. Don't play with that man's emotions, Maliah Michelle."

"I won't, mama," I promised. "And there isn't a woman on the planet who can break Murk's evil ass anyways."

She gave me a long look and then sighed as she stood up. "He still got you locked out the house?" she asked me.

"Yes, ma'am," I admitted sheepishly. "I haven't heard from him since he called to tell me that I could pick the kids up."

Rolling my eyes, I continued, "He got some nerve telling me when and where I can pick up my own damn kids."

"Well, it sounds to me like he's stepping into the role of a father, whether the two of you idiots have figured that out or not. Anyways, you can stay here until we get back," she told me. "You know the rules."

Nodding my head, I exhaled sharply and then stood up to kiss my kids goodbye. My mama was taking them to the beach in Jacksonville for a week and it took everything in me to keep myself from packing up and going with them.

"You out?" Candie asked me as I grabbed my things out of my locker and slammed it shut.

"Yeah, I'm not feelin' this shit tonight," I told her grumpily.

The kids had been gone for five days already and, during that time, Murk hadn't bothered to call me once. Tonight, I'd made so much money that I would make it to my goal in no time, but I couldn't even really celebrate because I was in a fucked up mood. I was horny and I was lonely but I didn't have anyone to help me out of my funk.

"Issues at home?" Candie questioned me.

I shook my head 'no'. She was cool and all, but I'd be damned if I let any of the girls know what was going on in my personal life with Murk. At the end of the day, we all had taken on a profession where we aimed to woo the biggest baller in the room at any expense. I didn't want to flaunt around the fact that Murk was possibly available for the taking.

"You know…I ain't seen Murk's sexy ass 'round here lately," Chyna chimed in after walking in the room.

She was covered with sweat, but her hand was holding a massive stack of money so her hard work had obviously paid off.

"What's up with that?" she asked.

"None of your damn business! Shouldn't you be worried about Tony?"

I eyed her angrily as she tossed back her head and laughed.

"Ain't no reason to get mean and shit, I was just asking a question! As for Tony…he ain't my nigga. We just have fun from time to time," she explained as if we really wanted to know.

"Well, Murk is my nigga so you can stop askin' about him," I informed her, feeling myself starting to get heated.

"If he is, he sure as hell wasn't actin' like it the last time he was in here."

I lunged for Chyna but Candie caught me and held me back with the help of another one of the girls who had just walked in the back after finishing her set.

They were quick, but not fast enough, and I'd managed to snatch off a piece of Chyna's weave before waving it over my head like a trophy and throwing it at her feet.

"You musky ass, monkey face bitch!" I shouted at her. "I'll fuck yo' stupid ass up if you try me again."

Smirking, Chyna grabbed her things out of the locker before leaving. Once she'd left, Candie and Diamond, the other woman who had held me back, let me go.

"You gone lose your job messin' with her. You know Tony don't go for that fightin' and shit," Candie told me.

I sucked my teeth and slammed my locker shut. "I ain't about to mess up my money for that zebra ass bitch. She ain't had no kids and I've had three, but she the one walking around with all them fuckin' tiger stripes going up and down her ass."

"Niggas be thinkin' them stripes make her look exotic," Candie joked, and I burst out laughing.

"I gotta go," I said, shaking my head at her crazy ass.

She waved bye and I walked out the back door. When I got to the car, I saw a figure move from behind it and I almost screamed until I saw who it was.

"Danny?! What the hell are you doing here?" I shrieked.

Unable to stop myself, I looked around quickly to make sure nobody, mainly Murk or his brothers, were standing around watching.

"I wanted you to see me so you could believe me when I say I'm better," he said as he stepped forward. "I'm getting back to the man I need to be for you and the kids."

"Danny, you can't be here!" I told him as my eyes continued to scan the parking lot.

A few people were standing outside, mostly men who were talking shit and smoking, but they didn't seem to be paying any attention to us at all.

"Li-Li, just look at me!" he said with urgency.

Finally, I allowed my eyes to settle on him and I gave him a really good look.

Damn, his ass is fine! I couldn't help thinking.

He had gained a little weight so he looked healthy, and it even looked like he had been working out a little. He had a fresh cut, was wearing clean clothes that looked fairly new and when he walked closer, I even picked up the subtle scent of his cologne.

"I caught a ride up here to see you so that you would be able to tell that I'm good. I need to be able to see you and my kids, Maliah. Stop running away from me," he pleaded as he looked sincerely in my eyes.

When he stepped forward and grabbed me around my waist, I swooned but then in the next second, backed away.

"I have to go now," I told him.

A few cars pulled up so I opened the car door and quickly ducked inside before I could be seen. Danny walked over and tapped on the window.

"Can I get a ride?" he asked.

Driving another nigga around in Murk's car was probably the easiest way to get my ass killed. I shook my head and Danny started to look frustrated. In the distance, I picked up on the loud rumbling of rap music being played through a custom-made speaker of someone's car, and I felt myself began to panic, thinking it was Legend. I cranked up the car and prepared to roll off.

"Maliah, just tell me where you're going!" Danny begged once more. "I'll meet you there…I just wanna finish talking to you."

The music began to get even louder. My thoughts merged in my mind as my heart started beating rapidly in my chest.

"My mama's," I said without thinking. "I'm going to my mama's house. Now get away before I hit your ass, Danny!"

With a sorrowful expression on his face, Danny stepped back reluctantly and I took off, tearing towards the road. I passed by Legend's car as soon as I exited the parking lot and we locked eyes as he pulled in. He didn't smile or make any expression at all once his eyes fell on my face, but I still felt my heart began to race. It wasn't until I was down the road that I finally began to breathe.

Something had to change. I had to get a grip on my life before I lost it.

They discover...

Chapter Sixteen

LEGEND

"Lil Nigga, why da fuck yo' monkey ass lookin' at me!" Gene shouted so loud making 10-year-old Leith nearly jump straight out of his skin.

"I wasn't lookin' at—I'm just tryin' to find my mama," Leith replied as he scratched at his arm nervously.

"Muthafucka, you ain't nothing but a little bitch ass mama's boy! She ain't here! She's with your ugly ass sister and Dame. Now what? You gone go somewhere and cry like the bitch ass muthafucka you is?" Gene spat, standing up from where he'd been sitting on the couch watching Cops with Quentin.

Leith glared at Gene with his jaw clenched, determined not to cry. Ever since he could remember, Gene had hated him because of who his father was. Dame, Quan and Quentin all belonged to Gene. Pablo's father was a Dominican man whom their mother had as a product of being raped and never spoke of. But Crystal and Leith's father was a man whom their mother loved more than any other man she'd ever known. Although Gene would abuse Pablo from time-to-time because he wasn't his, he never punished him as severely as he did Leith.

The boy's mother, Monice, met Leith Sr. after Gene had gone to prison for a drug and assault charge. Leith Sr. pursued her and Monice fell quickly in love with him, cutting off all communication with Gene whom she'd promised to wait for when he was sentenced to prison.

Shortly after their relationship began, Monice became pregnant with Crystal and not too long after, Leith followed. Leith accepted all of Monice's sons as his own and had their last names officially changed to match his: Dumas. Everyone seemed to love their family they'd created except for Quentin, who cried nearly every night for his 'real daddy'.

After doing eight years in prison, Gene was released and demanded that he be able to see his sons. Monice refused after Leith voiced his concerns with having Gene around them but, eventually she began to feel guilty about Quentin's constant questions about his father, and started sneaking him to see Gene behind Leith's back.

One day about three months after Gene was released from prison, Leith Sr. was working at the grocery store he managed when the store was robbed right before closing. In the process of the crime, he was shot and murdered. His death left a devastated Monice with six children, no money after burying him and growing bills.

Eventually, Gene convinced her that he was the one for her and she reluctantly allowed him back into her life, even though she still was heartbroken over Leith's untimely death. Gene knew that she didn't really love him and was only with him because she had no choice, and that angered him to the fullest. Therefore, whenever he felt he could get away with it, he'd take it out on Little Leith.

"Pops, please leave him alone," Quan pleaded after walking into the room. "He ain't do nothin'."

"Man, shut yo' ass up!" Quentin snapped at Quan. "Just mind your business."

Quan didn't respond but he walked over to where Leith stood, and posted up between him and Gene with his chin jutted out, ready to defend his little brother if he had to.

"Nigga, get your lil' skinny ass out the way!" Gene barked at his son with his hands squeezed tightly into fists at his side.

"No!" Quan yelled back at his father. "You not gone touch my little brother! As long as I'm around ain't nobody gone hurt my brother!"

"I ain't gone tell you no fuckin' more!" Gene bellowed. "Get out the fuckin' way!"

And with that, Gene reached back and knocked Quan out the way, making him fall onto the floor in an awkward position that bent his arm, nearly breaking it.

"Quan!" Leith called out and tried to run to him.

But before he could, Gene grabbed him by both of his arms, pinned them behind his back and lifted him in the air.

"You're hurting me!" Leith yelled out. Tears came to his eyes and he bit his lip to try to keep them away, but he couldn't, and they started to fall down his cheeks.

"What's going on?" Pablo asked, walking out of the bathroom in the hall just as Gene stormed by, holding Leith. "Wait…stop! Where is Dame?"

"Move out the fuckin' way!" Gene yelled, elbowing Pablo to the side and running into the boys' bedroom.

Slamming the door behind him, he locked it and then ran over to the bed, still pinning Leith's arms behind his back.

"Get off me! Leave me alone…get off me!" Leith cried out as he tried to fight.

"Shut the fuck up!" Gene yelled, punching him in the face as he held his wrists with his other hand.

Blood burst from out of Leith's nose and he began to see stars. He could hear his brother, Pablo, banging hard on the door, but the sound seemed to be so far away.

"Since you want to act like a bitch, I'mma treat you like a bitch!" Gene spat, making flecks of spit spot Leith's face as he tugged at his pants.

"Get off me!" Leith yelled out, a surge of energy coming into him as he realized what Gene intended to do.

"Lay still or I'll break yo' fuckin' neck!" Gene shouted back, squeezing Leith hard around his throat until he started to see black spots.

"That's right," he cooed when Leith stopped punching and kicking. His energy was gone because of lack of oxygen. All of the fight in him was gone and he was nearly unconscious.

"Be still…this won't hurt. Not too much…"

"Baby, wake up!"

Startled, I awoke in a cold sweat and reached out for my gun. It wasn't until Shanecia grabbed the sides of my face and pulled me so that I was looking into her eyes, that I realized where I was.

"You were having a bad dream," she told me with concern in her eyes. "You were talking in your sleep."

"What was I saying?" I asked her, feeling uneasy about the dream I'd had.

Memories that I'd worked hard to repress were coming back, and I wasn't prepared to deal with them. My past was fucked up to say the least, and I worked hard each day not to think on it. I always felt the need to prove to myself and my brothers how strong I was, and it was because of my bullshit past. Because of the things that happened to me, I felt compelled to act in ways that showed no weakness. Even though I knew they respected me as a man, sometimes I didn't feel that way because of what Gene did when I was younger and couldn't defend myself. The last thing I wanted was for Shanecia to find out about my past and I had to constantly prove myself to her too.

"I couldn't really understand…you were mumbling," she told me with a sigh. "The only thing I remember was 'get off me. Please get off me'."

Feeling the heat of fury rise of up through my spine, I turned away from her and clenched my jaw tight. Shanecia moved and tried to catch my eyes in her soft gaze, but I avoided her once more.

"Baby…is everything alright?" she asked.

"I'm fine!" I answered through clenched teeth, much louder than I wanted to. "I told you about asking me all these fuckin' questions, Neesy! If I wanted to talk about shit, I would!"

As soon as the words left my lips, I felt like shit. When I looked over at Shanecia, she had tears in her eyes that she was holding back. I exhaled heavily, letting out a deep breath, before turning towards her.

"I didn't mean to yell," I said, which was my version of apologizing. "I'm just stressed as fuck right now. What you got planned to do today?"

Standing up, I pulled on some sweatpants and grabbed my phone to see if I had any messages from my team.

"Maybe go over to Darin's to see Tanecia…I still haven't heard shit from my mama."

I nodded my head absentmindedly as I stared at the long list of missed calls I'd received from Dame.

The hell up with this nigga?

"Where your cousin? She coming back over here?" I asked her.

Shanecia shook her head. "Nope. I haven't—"

"Okay, well, you ain't goin' to Darin's today. You comin' with me," I told her.

"What?!"

Looking up from my phone, I gave Shanecia a hard look.

"You coming with me. It's the only way I can make sure that you're good. Shit is getting crazier so I need you with me. I don't want you alone."

She rolled her eyes and then turned around to get out of the bed as I stared at her. Her ass was rounding out and her thighs were getting thick as hell. When I met her, she ain't have all that meat back there, but a little bit of dick was plumping her shit up. Licking my lips, I checked the time on my phone to see if I could get in a quickie.

"No thanks!" Shanecia said as she walked into the bathroom. "I do not plan on living my life as your ride or die bitch. I'll pass!"

Frowning, I walked up on her just as she was about to close the door, and pushed it hard, slamming it back open.

"What da fuck you mean by that?!"

"I mean, I do not wanna be in the whip swerving up and down in these streets while you do what you and your roughneck ass brothers do! Plus, school starts back in a little over a month and I need to pick my classes and get my schedule together," she added as she began to brush her teeth.

Staring at her reflection through the mirror in the bathroom, I could tell from the way that she avoided my eyes that she knew full well she'd just dropped a bomb on me.

"School? You talkin' about Spelman?"

"Yes, Legend, that's where I go to college, remember?"

Walking up on her, I came all the way until my chest was just about touching her back, and looked down at her face from behind.

She tried to continue on as normal, but I could tell from the way her body grew tense that she knew I was about to nut the fuck up.

"What da fuck you mean 'that's where you go to college'? That's where the fuck you went to college before you became my woman! What you thinkin' right now? I know you don't think you going back to Atlanta!"

Shanecia bent down to rinse her mouth out, pushing her ass against my dick in the process. In spite of being heated, I felt it get hard.

"Legend, I can't just drop out of school because we are together!" she told me after she'd finished brushing her teeth. "We can have a long distance relationship or something and you can come and visit me. I'll come home during breaks or whenever I can."

Still avoiding looking at my face, she tried to slide past me but I stood my ground.

"You think I made you my chick and moved your ass in so I could be alone?" I asked, narrowing my eyes at her.

Placing her hands on her hips, she finally looked me in my face.

"Well, do you think I busted my ass to go to college so I could quit before I finish?"

"How about I bust your ass for even mentioning a long-fuckin'-distance relationship!" I shot back. I was heated. "Your educated ass do know we got schools right here in gotdamn Miami, right?!"

Sighing, Shanecia rolled her eyes and crossed her arms in front of her. She could cross her arms and huff and puff all she wanted to. She was going to have to figure out how to transfer her classes to somewhere in Miami, because I was going to call Spelman personally and tell them she wasn't bringing her ass back.

"Legend, you can't make me drop out of school just because we're in a relationship! This was something I was doing before you. And you're not my damn daddy!"

"Your ass be calling me daddy when I'm long-stroking that pussy!" I replied through my teeth as I grabbed my dick. "Don't make me drag your ass to the fuckin' room and remind your big head ass."

She batted her eyes a little and I knew she was getting wet although she was still trying to pretend like she had an attitude. I knew her ass better than she did.

"Dead that shit about Atlanta. You ain't goin' and that's it."

Before she could open her mouth to respond, the doorbell rang followed by loud knocks on the door.

"You expecting somebody?" I asked her. She shook her head 'no'.

Turning around, I walked to the door and looked out the peephole. Dame was standing right in front of the door, his big ass head taking up the entire view.

"What da fuck?" I said all of a sudden. "Is this nigga cryin'?"

Chapter Seventeen

SHANECIA

"You want some water?" I asked Legend's brother, Dame, as I walked in the room holding out a glass.

With red-rimmed eyes, he nodded and grabbed the water out my hand. My nerves were bad, so I popped a pill in my mouth and sipped from my own glass. Legend shot me a look but when I caught his eye, he didn't say anything.

"Neesy, you fam and shit, but you tell anybody you saw me like this and I'mma have to kill you," he said as he grabbed a Kleenex and blew his nose.

"Nigga, shut dat shit up witcho cryin' ass!" Legend shot back with the right part of his lip curled up as he frowned at Dame. "This some sad shit, yo. You a grown ass man and you over here snottin' and blubberin' about some shit you caused!"

A single tear slid down Dame's right eye and his lip quivered as he prepared to respond. I sat down on the arm of the chair Legend was in and stared at him pitifully. He looked completely and utterly devastated. I couldn't do anything but feel bad for him.

"I never thought she would leave me, man!" he said after wiping the tear away. "Trell is all I have. I love her! How could she just leave a nigga at a time like this?"

"A time like what, fool? You act like yo' ass dyin' or some shit. All you got is a STD. An STD that can be fixed with a prescription. An STD that yo' ass caught fuckin' around with them nasty bitches at the strip club. I told you to stop that shit."

I looked at Legend after he finished talking, feeling my heart warm at his words. Him saying that made me feel more confident that he'd never put me in the same situation that Dame had put Trell in many times before.

"Can you just call her for me? She won't talk to me but she always liked you, Leith. I just want to know where she is and make sure she's safe," Dame pleaded, his eyes glistening.

I bit my lip to stop myself from telling him that I knew where Trell was and that she was perfectly fine. She'd asked me not to say anything and I wanted to keep my promise.

"Hell naw, I ain't callin' her. I like Trell! Why the fuck I'mma call and ask her to talk to your pitiful ass? Be happy, nigga. Now you got the freedom to fuck all the nasty ass broads you meet. This should teach you that you don't shit where you sleep."

"You right, man," Dame said running his hand over his face in sheer distress and anguish. "I'mma get my shit together and get her back. I ain't fuckin' with no hoes. I'mma get my baby back and be a family man. I had me a good woman like you and I done fucked up."

Legend smirked when Dame called me a 'good woman' and cut his eyes in my direction.

"Neesy a'ight, with her five-head ass," he replied coolly. "But yeah, get your shit together because we gotta ride out. Murk is supposed to be on his way to scoop up the chick and he'll meet us at the warehouse."

With wide eyes, I turned to Legend but he jumped up and walked away almost like he knew that I was about to say something.

"Neesy, that goes for you too. It's time to go," he told me from over his shoulder as he walked away. "Grab them envelopes off the table and seal them for me so I can drop them in the mail."

Walking over to the table, I saw three envelopes open on the table. The first one caught my eye. It was addressed to the Chief of Police.

What the hell is Legend up to? I thought as I peeked inside. I saw a check for $20,000. So this is how he managed to never get into any trouble.

"You just had to be nosey, huh?" he asked me as he walked up behind me.

He was staring at me with a serious expression on his face but by his eyes, I could tell that he'd tested me to see if I would look and was disappointed that I'd failed. I shot him an apologetic look and rushed to seal the envelopes as he'd asked.

"Bring your laptop so you can decide which school you gone be at in August," he told me as he walked away. I sighed deeply and did as he'd requested.

Li-Li: *D is here.*

I gawked at the text and swallowed hard before I pecked out a response.

Me: *WHAT?!*

Li-Li: *He was sayin' he wanted to see the kids. Ima call you later.*

My heart sped up in my chest. I wanted to erase the messages but I felt Legend staring at the side of my face. I tried my best to neutralize my expression before he started to feel like something was up. Scrolling up, I saw there was a video she'd sent the night before but I was afraid to watch it while in the car with Legend. She must have sent it while I was sleep and it was bugging me that I hadn't noticed it until then.

Damn, Li-Li…what the fuck have you done?! I thought to myself as I pressed my lips firmly together and prayed that she wasn't doing anything stupid.

Legend looked away and I erased the last few messages as quickly as I could before I forgot.

We arrived at the warehouse about an hour after leaving the house and, for some reason I couldn't explain, I was nervous as hell about what I would see. It didn't take anyone to tell me, I already knew that the chick Legend had been referring to earlier had to be someone associated with Mello or his team and whatever Legend had in store for her wasn't good.

The sunlight blared into my eyes as soon as I stepped out of Legend's Escalade and placed my white Nikes onto the dusty gravel. Murk and Quan were standing on either side of the entrance to the warehouse looking like the soldiers they were, as they waited for their brother to arrive. Dame stepped out from behind me and he and Legend walked ahead of me as I nervously drug my feet to the door.

Legend walked in first, followed by Quan and Dame. Murk waited for me to walk in, nodding his head grimly as a greeting to me before stepping in and closing the door behind us. The warehouse was dark, nearly empty and cold. There was a metallic smell in the air that reminded me of something you'd smell in a morgue. Looking around, I wondered how many people had lost their lives in the very room I was standing in.

Legend pulled back a long metal partition that separated the room we were in from another area. As the door slid open, my eyes fell upon a woman, very attractive. She was hogtied to a chair with a dirty bandana in her mouth, gagging her to keep her from speaking or crying out. She was wearing a long loose-fitting, red maxi dress that was drenched with either sweat or piss. I couldn't tell, but what I could tell was that she was scared shitless.

Squatting down in front of her, Legend looked up into her eyes and the woman began to tremble viciously under his glare.

"You know who I am?" he asked in an icy voice that even sent chills down my spine.

Murk came up behind me and tapped me on the shoulder, nearly scaring the natural life out of me. I turned around and saw that he'd pulled up a chair for me. He motioned to it and I took him up on his offer, sitting down quickly. I didn't know what was about to happen but I didn't trust my legs to hold me up the entire time.

"I said do you know who the fuck I am?!" Legend repeated a little more forcefully.

The woman nodded vigorously, so hard that her loose, black curls framing her face, shook back and forth with her. Her eyes grew even wider than they had been before and filled with tears. I felt a pang in my chest as I thought about how scared she must have been. I'd been in her situation when Mello had taken me, so I didn't have to imagine how she must have felt because I'd been there.

"Then if you know who I am, you already know I don't give two fucks about you, right?"

Nodding her head, the tears began to slide down her face. I had to look away as my own eyes filled up with tears. I couldn't take this shit. Just as I was wishing that I'd played dead that morning so that Legend wouldn't have decided to drag me along with him, Dame nudged me and handed me one of the Kleenexes he'd had in his pocket.

"Here you go," he whispered.

"Thank you," I replied back quietly with a weak smile.

"No problemo, sis," he said back. "You just remember our secret."

He put his finger to his lips to remind me not to tell anyone about him crying earlier that day, and I almost giggled despite the situation in front of us.

"Yo' boyfriend, Montegro, is hiding and I want to know where he is," Legend continued. "If you tell me, you can go free, I promise. No need for you to be brave for a nigga…y'all ain't married and you ain't got no kids, so he really ain't shit. You gonna cooperate with me?"

My heart clenched in my chest as I waited for her to respond. The woman nodded her head and I let out a breath of relief.

"Okay, I'mma remove the gag. Then you better speak up quick, a'ight?"

She nodded again. Standing up, Legend pulled the gag out her mouth and she took a deep breath, gasping in gulps of air.

"I'm listenin'," Legend announced and stood in front of her, looking down at her as she tried to get herself together.

"He—last I heard, he's staying with his aunty. H—he left when you announced you was coming after Mello's team," she croaked out.

"Where does his aunty live?"

"Hollywood...she stays on Wiley Street. There is a bright green house over there...that's hers."

Legend looked at Murk who nodded his head and walked out of the warehouse.

"C—c—can I go now?" the woman cried out as she watched Murk walk away. "I—I told you what you wanted! That's all I know, I swear!"

"Naw, I don't think that's all you know. But you good for now."

Legend walked over and picked up her cellphone from a table in the room and began thumbing through it. Watching him, the woman looked like she was about to hyperventilate.

After a while, Legend frowned at something on the screen before placing the phone down and turning to Quan and Dame. He didn't say anything but the face he made told them his thoughts, and they both got up to follow him down the hall to another room.

As soon as they left, the woman's eyes focused in on me. I stirred uncomfortably in my chair and hoped that she would continue to act like I wasn't there.

"Hi...my name is Kendria. Please...c—can I just have some water?" she asked.

Frowning slightly, I didn't look up.

"Please? I—I'm pregnant and I'm scared that something is wrong with my baby. I'm so thirsty, I just need some water, please," she said again.

Shocked, I looked up at her, for the first time allowing my eyes to really take in her full appearance. Her dress was loose-fitting but the more I looked at her, I could see her round belly. She definitely looked pregnant. I didn't know how I'd missed that before.

"How far along are you?" I asked her, still staring at her stomach.

"Six months," she replied with her bottom lip trembling. "I'm just so thirsty. And scared."

I can't take this shit anymore, I thought to myself. *No woman deserves this.*

Standing up, I walked over to the small kitchenette area, grabbed a glass and ran some water from the faucet into it. Turning around, I walked towards Kendria, quickly hoping that she could hurry up and drink it before Legend returned.

Bending down in front of her, I held the glass to her lips and tipped it just so that she could drink.

"Thank you," she mumbled graciously.

She took a few sips and then I saw a flash of something to the side of my head. Seconds later, I felt a hard punch to one side of my face followed by a hard uppercut. The glass was snatched from my hand and I heard a crack as she slammed it on the edge of the table.

Recovering from the punches, I tried to catch my balance and fight but before I could, Kendria grabbed my hair and wrung it around her wrist. The next thing I felt was a jagged, sharp piece of glass to my throat.

"Hurry the fuck up and hand me that purse," she whispered into my ear. "Hurry up and don't scream or I'll slit your fuckin' throat!"

I swallowed hard and squeezed my eyes shut as she yanked even harder on my hair, pulling a few strands from my scalp. She had a vicious grip on me because she knew if I got away there was nothing she could do. She'd managed to get her hands loose from the rope but she was still bound by her ankles to the chair. She pressed the glass harder against my neck, cutting me enough to draw blood, but I still didn't move.

Kendria was asking for her purse but I wasn't stupid, and I'd watched enough Madea movies to know that she had more in there than lipstick and eyeliner. She was packing heat in it. If I gave it to her, I would certainly be dead and she would finish off Legend, Quan and Dame as soon as they walked in, unaware of what was going on. There was no way in hell I was getting it for her. If she was going to slit my throat, then so be it.

"Get the purse!" she urged again, yanking even harder on my hair.

Kendria moved the glass and sliced me across my chest, drawing more blood. It hurt like hell but it was a big mistake on her part. Moving the glass from my neck allowed me the freedom to move a little more.

Reaching up, I brought my arm back and delivered a hard elbow right to her midsection, hitting her in the stomach. She cried out in pain and released her grip on my hair, making me able to scurry away.

Two seconds later, Legend, Dame and Quan all burst into the room with their guns out and their eyes analyzing the scene before them.

"I'm fine!" I yelled out when I saw Legend's eyes focus in on the blood all over my body.

Bent down, Kendria was whimpering in the chair holding her stomach.

"The fuck happened?!" Legend asked me as he looked at the broken glass on the floor, the drops of blood and Kendria crying hysterically as she held her mid-section.

"She asked for some water…I gave her some and—"

"You untied her fuckin' hands, Neesy?!" Legend yelled.

"No, she was able to get her hands loose and then she broke the glass and—she had it to my neck and was asking me to get her purse. Th—there is a gun in there," I explained. The more I spoke, the dumber I began to feel.

How could I be so stupid? I thought to myself.

Legend gave me a look that made me wish I could crawl into a hole in the wall and stay there forever. I ducked my head down and my shoulders slumped. Out of the corner of my eye, I saw Legend lift his arm up. When I looked up, I saw he had his gun out and pointed at Kendria.

"Legend!" I called out. "No, she's pregnant!"

Staring at the side of his face, I could see his expression shift and I knew that, like me, he'd had no idea that she was pregnant. Quan looked up with his eyes wide and filled with horror as he stared at Kendria, his eyes pointed at her belly, before focusing in on Legend who was still holding his gun.

"Ah shit…" Quan cursed under his breath.

My thoughts merged as time seemed to slow to a complete stop while we all stared at Legend wondering what he was going to do, as Kendria continued to cry hysterically either from pain or as a last effort to try to preserve her life.

"She's pregnant, Legend!" I said again. "She was scared. You don't have to do this!"

Still looking at Kendria with his gun pointed, he clenched his jaw tight and I could tell that my words were getting to him. My heavy breathing was making the cut on my chest sting, as blood continued to spill from my wound. Grabbing the neckline of my shirt, I dabbed at the blood to clean it up. It wasn't a deep cut…only a warning slice. She hadn't caused any real damage at all. It probably wouldn't even leave a mark.

When I looked up, Legend's eyes were on me and his arm was down with his gun by his side. I breathed out a sigh of relief that he'd decided not to kill Kendria. I'd been in her position. She panicked and did something stupid because she was fighting for her survival. I would have done the same too, because I wouldn't have believed that Legend would let me go.

"I knew it!" a voice yelled out. It sounded dry, evil and almost deranged. It was Kendria.

"Mello always said you were nothing but a bitch ass nigga. Lil' fuck boy! You always do whatever your bitch says?"

My mouth dropped open as her words pierced my ears. When I looked into Legend's eyes, it looked as though they'd gone black. Turning around quickly, he lifted his hand up with supernatural speed and pulled the trigger three times, delivering a single bullet through her forehead and two to the chest. The force of the shots propelled her backwards and she fell to the floor with her dead eyes wide open, her mouth pulled into its final sneer and her lifeline oozing out of her skull.

Gasping, I covered my mouth as tears burned my eyes. Never in my life had I ever seen a dead body but here I was not just seeing one, I'd just witnessed someone being murdered right in front of my face.

"You not ready for this game you playin'!" Legend yelled at me. "I keep tellin' you that you don't run shit! When the fuck you gone learn?!"

"But you said you were going to let her go in the beginning. I just was trying to help her…I—I didn't know that she was going to say that!"

"That's my fuckin' point, Neesy! *You don't know*," he told me with less anger in his voice, but I could see he was still furious. "You grew up in the hood but you ain't grow up in the streets!"

Dame and Quan were sitting down with their heads down, trying to avoid looking directly over to where Legend and I stood. The awkward expressions on their faces made me feel even more like shit.

"Out of every fuckin' body in this room, you the only one who *actually* thought that I was gonna let that bitch go!"

Crinkling my brows, I looked up at him. "Wait…you weren't going to let her go?"

"Hell no! Lesson number 1 that you about to learn to-fuckin'-day: when you go to war with niggas, you don't save shit because it will always come back to bite you in the ass.

That bitch was a 'done dada'. I was gonna spare her just long enough to get your sympathetic ass out of the room so I could finish her off. She knew from jump that she wasn't goin' to make it out the room and that's why she tried you with that bullshit ass water trick."

Legend's phone rang and I was grateful for it because it took the heat off of me for a minute. Walking over, I sat down in my chair next to Quan and tried to keep myself from crying like the little, clueless girl I'd shown everyone I was.

"Aye, sis," Quan started as I sat down. "Don't take that shit to heart." He reached out to give me a dap. With a half-smile, I returned it.

"This kinda shit ain't for everybody. You and me…we got love for folks who don't deserve it sometimes. You kinda remind me of Cush. Legend used to yell at her about this same shit."

"Cush?" I questioned looking at him with a raised brow.

"Crystal," he answered with a look as if I should have known who he was referring to. "Our sister."

I was just about to follow up with another question when Murk's voice stopped me. Legend had put him on speaker phone.

"Aye, Murk, I got you on speakerphone…now what you said?" Legend asked through his teeth.

My breathing slowed as I waited to hear what Murk was about to say. Whatever it was, I could tell by the way that Legend was acting that it was bad news. I had a feeling that Kendria's dead body was probably only the first I'd see that day.

Chapter Eighteen

LEGEND

It was taking everything in me to keep myself from losing it. First, I saw something in that pregnant bitch's phone that looked suspect as fuck, then I walk in and see Shanecia covered in blood after doing some dumb shit. Next, I was forced to kill that bitch when I really wanted to torture the fuck out of her before annihilating her ass for calling me a 'fuck boy'. Last, Murk was giving me some information that had me questioning every decision I'd made in the last couple months.

"The word y'all gave was right. They knew we was coming after that bitch and these niggas already posted up, waiting to clap our asses as soon as we pulled up. The only thing I'm trying to figure out is...if they knew we was coming to get her, why didn't they just wait for us to grab her ass?"

That was a question I could answer easily.

"They wanted to get all of us and they didn't think I'd kill her, so it was a sacrifice they were willing to make," I told him, shaking my head sadly. "I told Alpha that I wasn't going to kill the women, just use them for information. Then I told him that we would run up on the rest of Mello's men as a team, so to be ready when I gave the call."

"This some fucked up shit," Dame muttered as he walked in closer. "So all this time you mean to tell me that this nigga was working with Mello?"

"It looks like it," I replied. "After I killed Sinai, he had to lay low for a while, but now his fuck ass is back doing what he does best."

"Yeah, and it looks like these niggas got our weapons, too," Murk said through the phone. "They out here heavy, carrying all kinds of shit."

"Murk, get the fuck outta there before them niggas see you," I told him, finally. "We got a lot of work to do. Alpha worked with our street team. Now we gotta figure out which of those niggas are loyal to us and which are not."

"A'ight. I'mma go holla at Maliah right quick and I'll be back 'round there. I wanna make sure she don't hit the club tonight. I can't take the chances of having some nigga grab her ass because they know we fuck around," he said.

"I understand. Get ya lady, nigga," I told him before hanging up the phone.

When I looked over at Shanecia, she looked sick in the face, but I figured it was because of everything that had happened the last couple hours. She'd had quite an initiation into the street life.

"How much does Alpha know?" Dame asked as Quan walked over to check our weapon and ammo supply.

"Too muthafuckin' much," I replied. "But we still good because we stuck to the code and kept most of the important shit just around the four of us. I've been swapping up our trap locations to keep niggas guessing. He don't know about this warehouse, he don't know where we stay, and he damn sure don't know where we keep our money or product. I regret trusting that nigga's weapons connect though. Something told me to get our own dealer."

Nodding his head, Quan walked over and said, "Yeah, but you can't blame yourself for that. We thought he was a thorough nigga. And we've known his ass forever."

"Wait…Alpha's the one who gave us the info on Sinai," Dame spoke up. "So you think Sinai was probably innocent?"

Silence loomed as none of us answered his question but we all knew the truth. Most likely Sinai was innocent and Alpha had used him as a scapegoat to cover his own ass. I needed a minute. It was hurting me to know that I'd killed one of the top members of my team and he was innocent.

I'd been so quick to believe Alpha because I was furious over the fact that Mello always seemed to be one step ahead of us. I knew Mello's stupid ass wasn't smarter than I was, so the fact that he was outplayin' me had me pissed off to the max.

When Alpha came with a little bit of evidence pointing towards Sinai possibly betraying us, I didn't hesitate to move on it. After all, Sinai had members of his fam who worked for Mello and he'd hidden it from me. When Alpha told me that, I couldn't help but believe that he'd been the one leaking information.

"We gonna have to figure this shit out and fast. I gotta know who we can depend on and who we can't depend on. Alpha will figure out soon that we know about him being part of Mello's team, so we gotta move fast."

Quan and Dame nodded their head and each of them pulled their phones out to start making calls. My eyes fell on Shanecia who was sitting in the chair with her shoulders hunched over as she pecked away on her phone.

"Who you textin'?" I asked with my brow lifted.

I didn't want to say anything too fast, but her ass looked suspicious as shit, ducked down in the corner texting and tried to cover her phone. Maybe it was everything going on with Alpha but I was wary of anyone at the moment, and she looked like she had secrets. When her head lifted up and an awkward expression crossed her face, I knew something was up. Then she did the one thing that I was praying she wouldn't do. Her eyes cut to the side, her cheeks went red and she licked her lips.

My heart clenched in my chest. I didn't know what she was about to say but I knew, whatever it was, it was about to be a lie.

SHANECIA

"I asked you who the fuck you textin'?!" Legend yelled at me and I felt a tickly sensation in my bladder as if I were about to pee on myself.

"I—um, it's just Maliah…I was just asking her about something about the kids," I told him, trying my best to give him enough information to drop the subject, but not too much for fear that I'd be the next dead bitch lying in the middle of the floor with a bullet through my skull.

Narrowing his eyes, Legend gave me a look that told me he didn't believe not a damn thing that I'd just said.

"Give me that muthafuckin' phone!" he demanded but before I could even do as he'd asked, he reached down and snatched it out of my hand.

I felt like I wanted to cry as he read my messages to Maliah. As soon as I heard Murk mention going over there to speak to her, my stomach had twisted up so bad that I thought I would throw up. If Murk ran into Danny while checking in on Maliah, I didn't even want to think about what would happen.

For that reason, I'd texted Maliah to warn her and I was happy I did because from her response, she was still trying to get Danny out of there.

"The fuck?" Legend cursed after reading the messages. I watched as he doubled back up and read them again.

"Danny? Ain't that her dead baby daddy?" he asked me, moving his eyes to my guilt-ridden face.

Silently, I nodded my head. He dropped the phone down in my lap and then stood in front of me with his arms crossed in front of his chest.

"Explain."

I licked my dry lips with a tongue that was just as parched, as I prepared to speak, hoping that I could piece enough of everything together to satisfy Legend and manage not to get Maliah killed.

"Danny—he's not dead. We thought he was…but the day Mello

grabbed me, he called me from the hospital and said that he'd had surgery and it had saved his life," I confessed.

"So she's been chillin' with baby daddy all this time is what you're sayin'?"

I shook my head. "No, he just recently proved that he's stopped using and he asked to see the kids, so I guess she let him visit them at her mama's house. She told me she was going to call me about it later."

"Did he say anything about the day he was shot?" he asked me.

Confused, I frowned as I answered his question, "No, he was too high to remember anything…"

My voice trailed off. I wanted to ask why he wanted to know, but I was positive that I didn't want to know the answer.

Legend gave me a long look and I felt myself getting angry at, once again, being in a situation where I'd felt like I had something to apologize for the second time that day. After a few minutes, he reached down and lifted my face up by my chin.

"I know that's your cousin and I know how you are about your family," he began looking me straight in the eyes. "But I'm the same way about mine. Warn your cousin that she better cut off all contact with that nigga ASAP. If I find out anything else about her and this nigga, I can't control anything my brother may do."

"But they aren't even really together!"

"Don't play stupid. Both of us know better than that."

He released my chin and I nodded my head sadly. My mind was racing as I thought through his words but I didn't say a word.

"Aye, I got something to tell you," he said only loud enough for me to hear.

On his face was an expression I'd never really seen before. He looked uncomfortable and awkward, for one of the first times since I met him. At that moment, he appeared more like a normal person with various feelings and emotions, instead of the ruthless, deadly leader that everyone knew and feared.

"What is it?" I asked.

Hesitating for a second longer, he bit his lip and then squatted down so that he was eye level with me as I sat in the chair. When he grabbed my hand into the both of his, I felt my heart began to thump hard in my chest.

"Neesy, I love you," he told me and my heart fluttered in my chest. "I've never told a woman that, ever. And because I love you, I want to let you know something." He paused and took a deep breath before letting it out.

"If you ever try this shit that your cousin is doing…If you ever even think about sneaking around behind my back with another nigga, I swear on my mama's grave, I will kill you and I won't think twice about it."

With that, he stood up leaving me trying to figure out whether to be happy about the fact that he'd finally admitted he loved me, or to be scared as hell over the fact that he'd threatened my life.

"Dame, Quan'll take you home. We out'chea!" he announced to Dame and Quan as he chucked them the deuces and then beckoned for me to leave with him.

"Your ass couldn't just tell me you loved me, huh Legend?" I snapped, standing up and punching him in the shoulder. "Leave it to you to threaten my ass in the process."

He chuckled and grabbed at his arm even though I knew damn well my little punch hadn't hurt him.

"You act like you ain't know your ass was fuckin' with a goon, Neesy," he told me as he slid his hand behind my back and around my waist.

"Oh, I know it," I replied with a shudder as my eyes fell on where Dame and Quan were wrapping Kendria's body up in some kind of large black plastic sheet.

"Well since you know it, don't ever forget it. Let that dead bitch over there be a reminder. It's better that you leave me before you betray me like that, got it?"

He gave me a look as we walked out the warehouse that was soft, but still showed just how serious he really was.

"I got it," I responded back, lacing my fingers in his. "Hey…how come you never told me about your sister?"

Stopping, Legend turned to me with a confused expression on his face as he tried to figure out what I was talking about. Then he sighed and ran his hand over his face, seeming mildly distressed.

"I have a sister, Crystal. We call her Cush. She's going to school in New York because I don't want her out here. It's not safe and she don't know how to listen. You'll meet her one day, but she has a way of pushing all of the women I deal with away. She's too protective of me and I'm not ready for her to be all in our mix yet."

I nodded my head, although I was still curious about this mystery sister of Legend's and wanted to ask more questions.

"How old is she?"

"We are nine months apart," Legend replied.

Instantly, I understood why she was so protective of him. She was probably closest in age to Legend and Murk, but Legend was the baby. Even though he didn't act like it, that didn't matter to sisters.

"Okay," I said finally. He opened my door and I sat down inside of the car.

"Just so you know it, I love your crazy ass, too," I told him before he closed the door.

"I already know it."

It didn't matter how crazy what he was saying sounded to me, I knew I would never let another man come in between what we had, so his threat wasn't really needed.

I was in love with him and there was nothing he could say or do that would change how I felt.

Chapter Nineteen

MALIAH

"Danny, you've got to go *NOW!*" I barked at him as I started throwing his clothes at his head.

Groaning, he clutched the sheets tight and pulled them up higher under his chin. Grabbing one of his shoes, I sailed it through the air right at his forehead. It connected before falling to the floor beside the bed.

"Li-Li! What da fuck, man?!" he yelled rubbing his head.

I snatched the covers from around him, exposing his naked body underneath.

"Oh my God!" I shrieked as I looked at another reminder of what must have gone down the night before. "You've got to get the fuck out of here right now!" I repeated.

I was in the most fucked up situation of my life and if Danny didn't get the hell out right that second, it would be the last situation I'd ever be in because I'd be a dead bitch. How the hell I'd allowed myself to mess around with his ass one more time was something I'd never figure out.

Well, actually, I could pretty much figure out *how* I'd allowed myself to sleep with Danny one more time. I didn't remember much about the night before, but what I did know was that I came home and made myself a drink to calm my nerves. Then some time later, Danny knocked on the door which reminded me that my stupid ass had actually told him where I was going before I left.

From there, the next thing I remembered was waking up with his ass in my bed and my panties on the floor.

Now how'd I allowed myself to sleep with his ass when I knew damn well that Murk and I weren't *technically* over was what I couldn't believe. Although we'd fought, we hadn't officially broken things off and, knowing what I knew about Murk, I didn't need an official title for him to still consider it cheating if I slept with someone else.

And with Danny on top of that! I hadn't even told Murk that Danny wasn't actually dead because I still wasn't completely sure that I believed he didn't have anything to do with him almost dying. Danny not being able to remember didn't make things any better.

"Li-Li, have you lost your damn mind? Why are you kicking me out like this? If yo' mama comin' back, it ain't that big a deal! Me and Ms. Loretta been cool!" he told me, throwing his hands up in the air. Leaning over, he reached for the covers so he could lie back down, but I snatched them further away.

"FOOL! This ain't 'bout my damn mama! Murk is coming over here and if he catches you in here, he will fuck the both of us up!"

A confused look crossed Danny's face as he worked my words around in his mind.

"Murk…you mean the D-Boy?" he asked.

"YES!" I replied, throwing his clothes at him to put them on.

"Why the hell is he coming over here?" Danny inquired as he pulled his shirt over his head.

He wasn't stupid. He was asking questions but he wasn't trying to sleep anymore either. One thing you could count on was that if Murk was coming over, he would definitely be strapped, and Danny didn't have anything on him to defend himself.

"Don't worry about all that. Just know he's coming," I mumbled as I tried to clean up the room as best as I could.

All of a sudden, I heard the sound of a car engine pulling up in the front yard. My body froze in place but my heart was knocking so hard against my chest that it was likely to pop the hell out and take off running on its own.

"SHIT!" I yelled running to the window.

Just as I'd expected, it was Murk pulling up in what looked like a brand new all-white Jaguar with pure gold rims. When I saw him park and cut off the engine, my blood went cold.

"Get your shit and hide in the fuckin' closet!" I whispered at Danny while picking up his things and forcing them into his open arms.

"I'm not gettin' in no fuckin'—"

"SHHHHHH!" I pushed him towards the closet. "Nigga, if you don't get your ass in there and hide, I promise you Murk is gonna kill the both of our asses *today*!"

Danny opened his mouth to say something but before he could, I opened the closet and shoved him inside. He lost his balance and stumbled back just far enough for me to pull the door closed. Then the doorbell rang and I instantly broke out into a cold sweat.

"God, please, if you get me out of this situation, I swear I will go to church every Sunday! I won't strip no more, Lord…I swear!" I prayed as I walked to the door, stopping by the bathroom for only a second to check out my appearance.

After fixing my hair and spraying some body spray to get rid of any smell of liquor and lust that still lingered, I walked to the front room to answer the door.

"What are you doing here, Murk?" I snapped as soon as I opened it. My heart was still slamming against my chest but I hoped that he wouldn't notice anything wrong.

Looking back at me with his soft, hazel eyes, he ran his hand over his perfectly groomed beard and sighed before responding.

"Maliah, you gotta move back in so I can watch after you and the kids. It's not safe out here," he told me.

His eyes raked my body as he spoke. I began to feel self-conscious and wrapped my arms around my frame to create a barrier between the two of us and give him less to scrutinize.

"What do you mean it's not safe?" I asked before I knew it.

Bitch, don't ask no damn questions! I told myself. *Tell that nigga 'okay' and let his ass go!*

"I mean that we found out somebody on our team has been working with Mello to double-cross us. A few people know that we mess around so that makes you vulnerable. You can't work at the club no more. It's too risky even with Jhonny watching over shit for me," he explained.

His eyes washed over my body again and then they stopped and his focus narrowed in on my neck. I felt myself begin to panic when he frowned.

"The fuck is that?" he asked as he squinted. "Is that a fuckin' passion mark? Some nigga been suckin' on yo' fuckin' neck, Li-Li?"

"What?"

I jerked at the collar of my night shirt and tried to pull it to cover the spot he'd been staring at. I felt my cheeks flush red and even though I was trying to hide it, I knew that he could see the guilt all over my face.

"How would I have a passion mark, Murk? I haven't done anything! It's probably just a bruise from dancing at the club."

His hard stare turned into a glare and I knew he didn't believe one word I was saying. My mouth began to get dry and my eyes started to dart around at my surroundings as I looked for an exit.

"Where are the kids?" he asked suddenly, catching me off guard.

"The kids?" I parroted.

He began looking behind me, trying to peek into the house. I felt my stomach jump and a nauseated feeling overcame me.

"They aren't here right now," I told him. My tongue made a sticky sound in my mouth as I spoke. It was dry and so was my mouth.

"My mama took them with her and she's not back—"

Before I could finish my sentence, a banging sound came from behind me. I gasped loudly as Murk pushed his way inside the house, pulling out his gun at the same time. Running my fingers through my hair, I walked quickly behind him trying to stop myself from acting like I had something to hide.

Unable to walk on my trembling knees, I stopped when Murk doubled past the kitchen table and I sat down in one of the chairs, hoping like hell he couldn't hear my knees knocking.

"Get the fuck up!" he shouted so loud I jumped straight up out the chair. "Bring your ass because if I find out you got a nigga in here, you already know what's up!"

Without saying a word, I got up and followed quietly behind Murk as he walked down the hallway. First he checked my mama's room as I watched him from the doorway. After examining every spot in the room that someone could possibly hide, he walked by me and through the hall to the other room. I was on his heels with my fists squeezed tightly by my side in anguish.

God, please! Every single Sunday…I'll turn my life around, I swear, I swear, I swear!

"Sit your ass in the middle of the bed," Murk ordered as soon as we walked into the bedroom.

I did as I was told and tried to blink back the tears that were tickling the back of my eyes. My mind was on my kids and my mama. What would they do without me? Who would watch after my babies?

"What I don't fuckin' understand is why muthafuckas still ain't smart enough to know not to try me like I'm a bitch," Murk mumbled as he walked around the room looking at every single thing as if he were trying to locate even the smallest hint of a man anywhere.

My eyes searched the room as well. I was hoping that I'd grabbed every bit of Danny's clothing and tossed it all in the closet with his ass. Just as I began to think that I'd managed to grab everything, my eyes grazed over a dingy white sock balled up in the corner of the room, only about six inches from where Murk was standing.

Gritting my teeth, I moved to stand up and kick the sock out of the way before he saw it, but when he took a step towards the closet, all of my focus went to him. Bile rose up in my throat and I tried to swallow it down past the lump that was also there, as I watched his hand grab the door handle.

You need to get the fuck outta here! my thoughts screamed in my head, but my feet were planted firmly in place like dead weights. My body was frozen in place as I stared with wide eyes at Murk walking into the large walk-in closet with his gun firmly tucked into his tight grip.

Suddenly, I saw him lift his weapon and point it in front of him as he flicked on the light switch in the room. A scream built up in my lungs as my mouth fell open, but it lodged in my throat as I mentally prepared myself to meet my maker right after Murk sent Danny to meet his.

I knew this was it. This was how it would all end.

Chapter Twenty

LEGEND

"Leith! Wake up! Leith!"

Startled, Leith jumped upright in the bed, nearly smacking right into Pablo who was standing above him. His entire body felt sore. Reaching down, he checked his clothing. He was fully dressed but he felt cold.

Maybe it was all a dream, *he thought to himself about Gene's assault.* Maybe he didn't do anything to me and I dreamed it.

"Get up," Pablo said once more. "Mama packed all of our things. We gotta get out of here."

"Why?" Leith asked softly, his eyes darting around the room as he looked for any sign of Gene. He felt comfort knowing that at least his mother was back home.

"I—I told her what happened to you," Pablo said. "I told her about Gene."

Suddenly, Leith began trembling uncontrollably as the realization that what he'd feared had actually occurred.

"It happened," he whispered to himself. "But I—I'm not even hurt down there. It doesn't hurt."

Pablo's face screwed up into a frown. "What doesn't hurt?" Leith ignored his question.

"Where is he?" Leith asked quietly.

Pablo's hazel eyes went black.

"You don't have to worry about him," he replied with his chin jutted forward.

Just then, Monice walked into the room, a rushed and tense expression on her face.

"Leith, Pablo...let's go!" she ordered them in a haunted tone as if she feared someone was after them. "Everyone else is in the car. Grab a few things and then we have to go!"

Confused, Leith didn't ask any questions, he simply did as his mother asked and looked around the room for the one thing that he wanted to take with him: his father's gold chain that he'd given him right before he was killed. Grabbing it up, Leith draped it around his neck and then followed Monice and Pablo out the room.

As they ran down the hall, Leith's head turned just as they passed his mother's room. Although the door was pulled partially closed, he could see something through the cracks of the door.

His mouth dropped open when he saw a figure on the bed that he recognized as Gene. He was lying on the bed with a pool of blood soiling the crotch of his khaki shorts...the same khaki shorts he'd had on the last time Leith had seen him. The ones he'd been tugging off his body right before Leith had blacked out.

Also bloody was his bare chest. Leith squinted through the cracks and saw what looked like long punctures in various spots on his chest and stomach. It looked like he'd been attacked with a butcher knife.

"Leith!" Monice called, pulling his attention from the door. "Let's go!"

When Leith turned around, his eyes fell on Pablo who was standing a little ahead of him looking at him with his hazel eyes dark, cloudy and hooded. It was at that moment that Leith understood what had happened and knew why they were leaving so suddenly. It was then that Leith understood the true meaning of family and brotherhood.

"No change," Shanecia said, as she walked in the room wiping tears from her eyes. "I hate seeing her like this. She's losing so much weight. She doesn't even look the same!"

I tried to push the memories of my past from my mind, and wrapped my arm around her when she sat down next to me. She fell into me and I rocked her gently. We were at Darin's house visiting Tanecia, who was still in a coma.

I hadn't seen her since the day I found her nearly dead and fighting for her life because of the attack I'd ordered on Mello's crib. Although she shouldn't have taken her ass over there no way, I still knew it was fucked up to have to tell Shanecia that her sister was in a coma and would probably die because of me.

As much as I knew Shanecia wanted her sister back, I couldn't help but hope that her ass would stay just the way she was long enough for me to figure out a way to explain or at least suffer some kind of memory damage the way that Danny supposedly had.

Just thinking about that nigga still being alive and having dealings with Murk's lady friend, had my mood fucked up. I'd never, not even once, betrayed Murk, but I felt like I was coming mighty close to it for not saying anything about Danny being around his girl. Kids' father or not, if any nigga is around my chick, I wanna know and I wanna be there to keep tabs on that shit.

Shanecia swore that Maliah was only allowing Danny over to see the kids. I believed her when she promised there was nothing else going on between Maliah and Danny, so I'd keep the fact that he had been around her a secret for now.

As for the fact that he was still alive…I would be delivering that news to Murk ASAP so he could finish the job. There was no way in hell that I could allow him to keep his life at this point. He was a loose end that could later come back and become a major fuckin' problem.

"Let me get you home," I told Shanecia as I breathed in her sweet scent. "It's been a long day."

Without saying a word, she nodded her head and slowly stood up. I watched as she walked back down the hall, probably to tell Darin goodbye. I had to give it to that nigga, he was in love with Tanecia and more dedicated than any dude I'd ever seen. If it had been me in his predicament, I would have chucked her ass the deuces. I couldn't promise loyalty to those who couldn't give it back to me.

When Shanecia emerged from down the hall, she was wiping

away tears again and I felt my chest get tight. Thanks to me, she was pretty much all alone. Her mama was strung out on drugs that I'd gotten her hooked on and her sister was in a coma that I'd put her in. She didn't even have Darin anymore because he wouldn't leave Tanecia's side, and Maliah was one stupid decision away from getting permanently dealt with.

I was all she had but every single day, I was living a life that could lead to my demise with only one wrong move. Every day I walked out the front door accepting the fact that I may not walk back in it. But all I knew was the streets so I didn't have a choice in the matter.

Seeing the expression on Shanecia's face as she began to accept that Tanecia wouldn't make it through, was killing me on the inside. Mainly because the more she accepted that she was losing her family, the more I could see her growing closer to and relying more on me.

But was I really enough for her? Could I even be the man for her? And what would happen to her if anything happened to me? The streets could take me at any time and then who would she be left with then?

Chapter Twenty-One

MURK

The feeling pumping through my body was one that was foreign to me. It was an emotion I hadn't felt since I was a little boy: fear.

As I walked all over Maliah's mama's house searching for a nigga that I prayed wasn't there, I was fearful, for the first time in forever, of what I would do to her if I found him. As much as I denied saying it, Maliah had heard it and I did, too. I told her I loved her and I really did. But if she was hiding a nigga in this house, I wasn't sure how I would react but it wouldn't be good.

I grabbed the doorknob for the closet and swung it open wide, with my gun pointed in the air. Peering through the dark, I was almost certain that I saw something. I turned on the light and took aim as my heart thumped loudly in my ears.

Closing my eyes, I let out a breath and dropped my gun to my side when I saw there was nothing there. The closet was empty. A feeling of relief flooded through me and I took a moment to collect my thoughts before turning around to face Maliah.

When I turned around, Maliah was still sitting on the bed with a ghastly expression on her face. Her complexion was uncharacteristically pale as she waited for me to speak.

"No one in there," I said finally, kicking at a cup that was on the floor. "So tell me again how you got that thing on your neck?"

"I don't know, I'm just guessing I got it from the club because that's the only place I'm at other than here," she answered weakly.

"Aye." I nudged her with my index finger. "If somebody did something to you at the club, you need to tell me. Ain't no need to be trying to protect niggas because I'm a find out and fuck his ass up."

"Nobody did anything," she said. "I didn't even notice the mark was there until you mentioned it."

I felt my phone vibrate in my pocket and it was what I needed to remember the reason I'd driven over there in the first place. My eyes went back to the mark on Maliah's neck. It was small and faint, but it was definitely a bruise. How the hell she'd gotten it, I wasn't able to prove just yet, but one thing I knew was that sooner or later, I always came out on top. If she was up to some bullshit, I would find out.

"Get your stuff and let's go. You can leave most of this shit because most of your clothes are still at the house," I told her. "When will the kids be back?"

"I have to call my mama and ask her," she said as she moved off the bed and started pick up a few of her things around the room.

I watched her as she moved around cautiously as if she were uncomfortable or fearful that something would go wrong at any moment. My instincts were telling me something wasn't right. While she collected her things, I started walking around the house again, doubling back to make sure I'd checked out everything.

"Are you ready?"

Turning around, my eyes fell on Maliah as she walked to where I stood and gazed up at my face.

"Yeah, let's go."

Chapter Twenty-Two

SHANECIA

Legend had gotten his way as usual. Although I hadn't officially withdrawn from Spelman, I was heading over to Florida International University to see if there was any way I could transfer my classes in time to attend school that Fall.

Everything I was doing was last minute and to get into any of the schools of my choice was nearly impossible. But Legend told me to pick a school, get the information and he'd see about the rest, so here I was.

"There are a lot of fine ass niggas on this campus," Maliah observed as I parked in front of the admissions office. "Look at them with their educated asses lookin' like doctors, lawyers and insurance agents! Maybe I need to go to college."

I cut my eyes at her and sucked my teeth. "Maybe you should remember the situation that you're already in before you go adding to your pile of bullshit."

Casting her eyes downward, Maliah nodded her head and then turned to me.

"I really thought he was gonna kill my ass, Neesy," she said in a grim tone. "I still don't know how that nigga got out the house in time!"

"You haven't heard from him?" I asked.

She shook her head. "He's been calling but I haven't been answering. All I know is I need to go to the store after this to get me a job because I'm taking my black ass to church on Sunday."

"You need to go home tonight, sit down and explain everything to Murk ASAP. Skip the part about the drunken sex, but he needs to know Danny is alive. You can't keep the kids away from him and you can't keep sneaking around. If Murk cares for you and the kids, he'll find a way to understand."

A quick game of tug-or-war commenced on her face before she finally allowed herself to smile.

"You always was the smart one in the family." She rolled her eyes. "What I'm afraid of is, if Murk had something to do with Danny getting shot, if I tell him he's alive, how do I know he won't go back to finish the job?"

She had me there because I'd been thinking the same thing a few times before. Then I thought about Legend and what he always said to me.

"If you're going to be with him, you have to be able to trust that he will do whatever is right for you and the kids and leave it at that."

Maliah stared at me for a minute before her face broke out into a smile.

"I hate your smart ass!" she giggled. "But you're right. Let's go and get finished here so I can get back and figure all this out with Murk."

The entire process was quicker than I thought it would be. Mainly because everyone kept telling me the same thing at first: I was too late and there was nothing they could do. Finally, I spoke to a black woman who was the receptionist to an admissions advisor, and she put me up on game. I could take one class at the local community college and then transfer into FIU in the middle of the semester. It wasn't what I preferred but it would work, and Legend would be satisfied that I didn't have to leave.

"Let me go to the bathroom and then we can go," I told Maliah as I ducked into the restroom.

After I was done, I walked back out but Maliah wasn't in the place she had been before. Scanning my surroundings for any sight of her, I began strolling the hall. Suddenly, I began to feel like I was being watched and I snapped my neck behind me to look around. Just as I did it, my eyes fell on who it was watching me, just as he turned and began walking brusquely away in the opposite direction. I recognized who he was instantly. He looked just like Quan.

"Quan!" I yelled out and waved. But he didn't turn around.

Legend thinks he's slick, I thought to myself. *So you let me go to check out the school on my own but you make Quan follow me, huh? I got your ass, Legend.*

I started to jog after him but right at that moment, Maliah came up and grabbed my arm.

"What's wrong? You good?" she inquired with her brows bunched together in concern.

"Yeah, I just saw Quan. Legend got him following us," I told her and rolled my eyes. "I guess he still thinks I can't take care of myself."

"He's just makin' sure you're safe and after you got snatched by Mello, I don't blame him. That time was a warning that he needs to be more careful. If anything happens to you again, it'll be on him," Maliah explained to me.

Smirking, I cut my eyes at her as we walked to the car.

"What?" she questioned with wide eyes. "Listen, you may know all that Dr. Phil shit you was telling me earlier because of your classes at Spelman…but I know this street shit. So let me school you."

Looking at her, I laughed as we got in the car, but I knew she was right.

Chapter Twenty-Three

LEGEND

No matter what was going on in the hood, it was Saturday, so I was about to take my ass right to the rec center like I did every damn week. Wasn't nothing about to stop me. That was my routine and I was sticking to it.

At the same time, mama ain't raise no fool. The D-Boys were at the rec center but so was our entire team of hittas, and them niggas were strapped up to the max. We never had been the type to deal with a lot of people one-on-one, and no matter how many territories we took over, it would stay the same.

Out of the entire team of men under our control, only five, including Alpha, spoke directly with us. Each of the five headed up their own teams and, as long as the money matched up at the end of each week, all was good. Now that Alpha was gone, I was down to four and had to find a quick replacement. It was going to be tough, seeing as I'd just replaced Sinai.

"Nigga, what the hell is that you reading?" Murk asked. "Is that the same damn book from before?"

Stuffing the phone in my pocket, I gave him a sideways look and said, "Man, mind yo' business. We got work to do."

It wasn't the same book. I'd finished *Beloved* a while back right before my flashbacks had started. After breaking into Shanecia's Kindle account, I'd found something else to read but I wasn't about to tell Murk's ass what it was so he, Dame and Quan could laugh they asses off at my expense.

"What about Smitty?" Murk asked me as we looked around at all of the men spread out around the outside of the rec center. I leaned back on the hood of my whip and took a swig of my Heineken before shaking my head.

"He would be good, but don't nobody respect his ass because every damn body done fucked his bitch behind his back," I told Murk who nodded his head.

"Yeah, she was tryin' to give me the eye the other day. Ain't that some shit?" he replied.

"If *she* don't respect his ass, ain't nobody else gonna," I said.

"I was havin' Jhonny watch Maliah out at the club. He might be good," Murk offered. "He's loyal and people respect him. Ain't never been no problems and he stay low-key...ain't flashy or no shit like that."

My eyes traveled over to where Jhonny was posted up on the wall as he scanned the crowd. He did seem like he would fit and I knew for a fact that we could trust him. He'd started with us when he was around our same age and, even though he did his own thing, he was always there when we needed him.

"I'll think on that."

Suddenly, a car pulled up that I recognized. Reaching down, I immediately went for my weapon.

"I know that ain't who the fuck I think it is," I mumbled under my breath.

At my side, I saw Murk go for his banger as well.

"Dead muthafuckin' nigga walkin'," he replied, thinking the same thing as me.

Seconds later, Dame and Quan came up by our side, both of their eyes planted on the car. The door opened and we all waited for a head to pop off so we could decide if it was time to start blasting. But, although we were all expecting to see Alpha, that wasn't who stood up out of the front seat. It was Omega.

With my piece still in my hand, I frowned deeply and kept my eyes on Omega, wondering whether or not I should bring down on him the same judgment I was reserving for his brother.

The only thing that stopped me was that Omega was a kid at only sixteen. Alpha was the oldest and Omega was the youngest of the three boys. I didn't know who the middle brother was because he'd gotten killed out in the streets before I met Alpha. On top of his age being an issue, Omega had never been in the streets. Although all of the men in his family had died in the streets, with the exception of his brother Alpha, Omega had chosen to put his attention into basketball instead.

"Legend!" he called out as soon as he saw me.

His long, lanky legs took off in a run as he came into my direction and, within seconds, all three of my brothers had pulled out their weapons and held them to their side.

"Slow yo' roll, lil' long neck nigga," Murk warned. "What's yo' beef?"

Planting his feet in the ground, Omega put his hands in the air in surrender.

"I ain't got no beef," he informed us all. "That's why I'm here."

Narrowing my eyes, I studied him for a few seconds before nodding my head.

"Go 'head."

Licking his lips, Omega came in close and prepared to speak. Although my brothers relaxed, they all kept their eyes on him just in case.

"I just found out some shit about Alpha and what he's up to...he came to talk to me yesterday but he was actin' like it was the last time I was gonna see him. He told me he been workin' with Mello and gave me his car before he took off..."

I could see Omega was visibly shaken and seemed to be battling between talking to us or protecting his brother.

"…I just came here to say that I'm not part of any of this street shit. Never have been and I never will. I appreciate everything y'all done for me when it comes to the game," he said referring to the donations I'd given him to play, "but this street shit ain't me. But I want to ask y'all to spare my brother. H—he ain't thinkin' straight and I could tell somethin' ain't right."

Ahhh, shit, I thought and cut my eyes to Murk. *Here we go.*

Omega was about to beg us to spare his brother's life and that was one thing that was not gonna happen. Alpha made his decision and he had to pay for what he'd done.

"…When he was walkin' I could tell somethin' just wasn't right. He would never betray y'all…somebody must be makin' him do it," Omega finished.

Reaching up, I rubbed my hand over my head before looking at him.

"Mega, the best thing for your brother to do right now is to stop hidin' so we can talk to him. I can promise you that I'll give him the chance to explain himself," I promised, making sure to choose my words carefully.

It seemed to be enough for Omega because a smile crossed his awkward looking face and he nodded his head.

"Thank you, Legend. That's all I ask…somethin' isn't right and I just want him to be able to explain," he told me.

"I promise I'll let him explain," I said again.

Omega grinned once more before turning and walking away, pulling off his sweatshirt as he trekked towards the rec center wearing his jersey.

As soon as he was in the building, Dame and Quan walked away leaving me and Murk still leaning on the car.

"Get the fuck away!" I heard Dame yell all of a sudden. When I turned to look at him, he was waving away Brisha, a chick that he'd messed around with in the past. Thinking he was playing, she reached out to grab his arm but he ducked away.

"I said, get the fuck away! I'm a one bitch nigga for life. Bye, bitch," Dame announced stiff-arming her out of the way.

"Yo, that nigga crazy." I laughed as I watched Dame walk away from the thirsty chicks staring at him.

"Yeah, but he ain't slipped up yet though...Aye, you think that lil' nigga gone be a problem?" Murk asked me.

"I don't know but I like Omega," I said, lighting up a Black 'n Mild.

Murk nodded his head and said, "Yeah, he's become like hood royalty since he been ballin' and shit. If we would have had a lil' Mega when we were growin' up, we might have chosen somethin' else other than this street shit."

With the cigar between my lips, I began to laugh and Murk shot me a confused look.

"What the hell you laughin' at, nigga?"

"Pablo, you know yo' lil' half-Mexican ass can't play no fuckin' ball!" I laughed louder, knowing that he was gettin' pissed off at being called Mexican when his dad was supposedly Dominican.

"Nigga, my donor was Dominican, not Mexican," he corrected, punching me in the shoulder before snatching the cigar out my hand. "Fuck you and fuck that nigga."

"Aye, on some real shit tho', I need you to follow Mega for a lil' bit. Just to make sure that he good. I like that nigga but I can't underestimate him," I told Murk.

Nodding slowly, he thought on my words.

"You right. As much as I don't think he involved in this shit with Alpha, we've seen crazier shit."

SHANECIA

"Neesy!"

"Hmm?" I groaned into the phone as I tucked my pillow more comfortably under my head.

What time is it? I thought to myself as I yawned. It felt like it was too-damn-late-for-niggas-to-be-calling-me o'clock.

"Neesy, she just woke up!" Darin's excited voice poured in my ears through the speakers. "She just woke up and she's asking for you!"

"What?!" I yelled snatching the covers off my body and tossing my legs over the side of the bed. "Tan's awake?!"

"Yes, she is." I could hear him smiling through the phone as I stuffed my feet into some sneakers. "She's still a little weak, of course. But she's speaking. She's awake!"

"Okay, I'm on my way. But listen…I haven't showered or brushed my teeth or combed my hair or anything, so don't say shit. I'll bring my stuff and do all of that when I get there."

Darin laughed and it felt good to hear him sound like normal.

"I understand, Neesy. I ain't worried about all that shit. Your sister is awake and she wants to talk to you so bring your dirty ass over here."

He didn't have to tell me twice. I grabbed a duffle bag and started running around the room, tossing everything I needed inside. Although Legend had been home when I fell asleep, he was nowhere to be found, which wasn't a surprise. He always tried to make it home to be with me, at least until I fell asleep, if he knew that he was going to have to be out all night.

After sending him a quick text to let him know where I was going, I grabbed my bag, locked up the house and jumped in the car. The ride to Darin's house was about a fifteen-minute drive, but I was determined to make it in a little over five.

***

"I look like shit, don't I?" Tanecia queried as soon as I walked in and stood by her side.

Smiling, I ran my hand over the top of her head.

"As soon as you get up we gotta do something to this head of yours but other than that, you're good," I joked before sliding in the chair at her bedside.

Both of our eyes teared up at the exact same time as we began to get emotional. The nurse attending to her scribbled something in her chart and then slid out of the room to give us some privacy.

"I know what I did was stupid," Tanecia admitted and then bit down on her bottom lip. "I knew while I was doing it that it was stupid. But I wanted to believe that I could have a baby and give it more than what we had…you know?"

Shaking my head, I leaned over and grabbed her hand, enclosing it in mine.

"Tan, what we had wasn't all bad. We grew up fine. You keep going after these men who don't care about you and look what happened! He almost killed you, Tan! He killed your baby!"

Furrowing her brows, Tanecia scrunched her face up at me as if I were speaking a foreign language.

"What do you mean *he* almost killed me? Are you talkin' about Mello?"

Blinking rapidly as I ran through my thoughts once more, I sat back in my chair and slowly started nodding my head.

"Yes, Mello...he's the one who shot you, right?"

Tanecia's frown deepened on her face as she pulled away from me and gazed into my eyes. A chill ran down my spine as I waited for her to speak. My hands started to feel hot and clammy.

"No...he didn't shoot me," she stated. "But I know who did."

They learn...

Chapter Twenty-Four

LEGEND

Walking into Darin's house after receiving a 9-1-1 text from Shanecia had me on edge, but I was ready to take whatever was about to be thrown at me. The first blow was when she told me that her sister was awake. The second blow was the last text she'd sent me telling me to get over there as quickly as I could.

So, naturally, I took my time getting there, making a couple stops on the way before I pulled up to Darin's crib to see what was up. No less than two seconds after making my entrance, Shanecia ran into the living room and came right at me.

"Well damn, finally!" she miffed. "You couldn't have possibly taken any longer."

Confused, I scratched at my jaw. She grabbed me by my wrist and began pulling me down the hall towards the room that Tanecia was in.

"Tan knows who shot her," Shanecia announced as we walked towards the room.

Tugging her back, I stopped before we went any further.

"Neesy, let me explain real quick," I began. She whirled around with her mouth open to say something but I stopped her.

"I didn't know Tan was in the house when we raided it. She wasn't supposed to be fuckin' with that nigga no more! The last place I would think her ass would be was in his spot. You can blame me for a lot of shit but you can't blame me for the stupid ass decision she made!"

"What?" Shanecia asked. She searched my eyes with a frown and I could see her thinking back through everything I'd said.

"Tan said she was shot twice by Mello's wife…what are you talkin' about?" she asked finally.

Stunned, I froze in place for a few minutes before stuffing my hands in my jean pockets and licking my lips.

"Shiiiiidddd, I'on even know. I'm high," I shrugged.

"Legend, stop playin' around! This is serious!" Shanecia chided as she turned around and walked into the room at the end of the hall.

Breathing out a sigh of relief, I came in behind her still trying to figure out how in the *hell* I was able to come out of this situation this easy. Sometimes I felt like God knew a nigga had been through a lot, so every now and then he would shed some grace on my ass.

Inside the room, Tanecia looked better than what Shanecia had described to me during the days before, but far from herself. Darin nodded his greeting to me when I walked in the room and Tanecia gave me a weak smile. Nothing about how she was acting indicated that she remembered seeing me the day she'd gotten shot. So far, so good.

"Tan says that Mello's wife shot her," Shanecia repeated. "And the lady I told you about at the hospital that one day? I think that was her."

Slowly, I nodded my head and began to wonder why I'd been sent a 9-1-1 text to rush over here just for that little tidbit of information.

"She looks like a white chick…I saw him with her before but I didn't know she was his wife. I met him at his place thinking he wanted to meet with me but it was atually his wife who had texted me from his phone. She showed up while I was in the bedroom…we argued and she shoot me."

Suddenly embarrassed, Tanecia's face flushed red, as tears came to her eyes, and she ducked her head down. Checking my watch on my wrist, I shuffled my feet and cleared my throat. There was a lot left for me to do and I needed to meet up with Murk to discuss the situation with Omega. I couldn't see the reason why I needed to be here.

"Anyways," Tanecia continued with a sigh. "I know where she stays and I'm ready to give you the address. I'll help any way I can so you can do what you need to do."

Now the trip here was starting to be worth my while. Stepping forward, I pulled out my iPhone so that I could record the address. She rattled it off to me and I nodded my head in thanks. Her lip quivered and for some reason, I thought I should say something.

"You're doing the right thing," was all I could think of.

Thankful, she looked up and nodded her head as Shanecia beamed at me and grabbed my hand in hers. It seemed like I'd said the right thing but I shrugged like it wasn't nothing. But secretly, I was feeling myself for getting better at this boyfriend shit.

"I know...at first I didn't want to get involved and feel responsible if anything happened. But after losing my baby, almost losing my life and hearing what happened to Shanecia..."

She stopped talking and I felt like it was my turn to say something comforting.

"I understand," I inserted. Shanecia nestled her breasts against me which let me know I'd said the right thing once again. I kissed the top of her head and then tapped her on her lower back as I moved out.

"I'll call you," I told her as I walked out.

"I wanna move on this tonight," I told Murk as I sat in the car, speaking to him over the Bluetooth.

"Bet," he replied. "I'm about done with the lil' mission you had me on so I'mma head back to the crib in a bit. The kids finally back in town so Maliah's mama is moving into one of the guest rooms."

I'd just started driving and my eyes were on the road but something he said to me didn't sound right.

"The kids are back in town? I thought they been with y'all?" I questioned. "How long they been gone?"

"About a week, I think. I'm not too sure. They were already gone the day I went to tell Li she had to move back in."

"FUCK!" I cursed angrily and punched the steering wheel.

Either Maliah had lied to Shanecia or Shanecia had lied to me. Either way, I knew I was on some bullshit when I told Shanecia I wouldn't let Murk know about Danny and it hadn't even been but a few days later and I was already finding out my instincts were right.

"What, Legend?" Murk asked when I didn't readily explain what was going on.

"That day you went over there, I caught Neesy texting all in the cut on her phone. So I snatched that shit up to see who she was texting. It was Maliah."

"Yeah...and?" he inquired further.

"She had sent Neesy a text saying that nigga Danny was over there. When I asked Neesy, she had this long ass story about how he wasn't dead and blasé, blasé...said that he was over there just visiting the kids."

"Danny...you mean her baby daddy?" Murk asked.

"Yeah, I thought you clapped that nigga!"

"I *did*!" Murk replied before pausing for two beats. "But I was rushing because I had to meet y'all at Mello's spot. I didn't wait until the end to see that shit through. That was my mistake."

"Well, my mistake is that I didn't tell your ass this shit right when I found out."

"It's all good, bro," Murk said in a flat tone.

I knew his mind was already working on some shit that wouldn't be good at all for ole girl. Whatever he did wasn't my concern. She made her decision and she had to deal with that.

"I always got your back, Murk," I affirmed. "Listen, we ain't never talked about this shit but it's been fuckin' with me lately. Especially now with finding about what Maliah was really up to...I don't want you to think I don't have your back with this shit."

I paused and pressed my lips together, wondering if I should just drop the subject all together.

"You know when Gene...when he did that shit to me—I keep thinking back to how you got rid of that nigga for me. No matter what happens I know that you always got my back."

A long pause followed before Murk finally spoke up.

"Legend...I didn't kill Gene," he replied slowly. "You did."

"What?!" I shouted, nearly swerving off the road. I pulled over to the side and threw the car in park.

"Nigga...you tellin' me you don't remember that shit?" Murk asked me.

Closing my eyes, I thought back to that day but came up blank on what occurred before I passed out.

"Naw, bro...I passed out and you was tryin' to bust down the door. I woke up and mama was tellin' us we had to leave."

After delivering a long sigh, Murk started to speak.

"Man, I wish I could take credit for clapping that nigga, but it wasn't me. That fuck nigga had you so tight around your neck, you'd almost blacked out by the time I busted up in there. I had to grab a butcher knife from the kitchen to slice up the wood panel and help me break down the fuckin' door.

When I got in, that gay ass nigga was standing in front of you with his dick out, holding you by your fuckin' neck. He let go when he saw me and you fell out coughing and shit. As soon as he took a step in my direction, I sliced his shit straight off with the knife and he dropped to the floor, holding onto where I cut it. Blood was every fuckin' where! I was scared as hell and dropped the knife. Then you jumped up, picked it up and started stabbing the shit out of that nigga. After you were done, you laid down in the bed and passed the fuck out. Me, Quan and Quentin drug his ass into the room and put him in the bed. When mama came home... well, you already know."

I gritted my teeth and squeezed my eyes closed as I listened to what Murk was saying, small fragments of the memories beginning to slowly resurface in my mind.

"All this time, I thought Gene had—I really thought he'd …" I stopped, unable to finish my sentence.

"Hell naw," Murk replied, knowing what I was thinking. "It ain't go down like that. You bossed up on that nigga and you been carrying the fam on your back from that day on. Ain't none of us want to be dealin' with Gene! Not even mama. You was the only one who had the guts to get rid of that nigga."

"With you by my side," I added, pulling back on the road.

"And that's where I'll always be, fam," he promised. "Listen, I'm about to handle some business and I'll hit you back later on."

"Bet," I told him and ended the call.

I placed two fingers to my lips, kissed them and then pressed the same two against my father's gold chain that I kept around my neck. Deep down, I knew that Gene had been the man who killed him. To know that I'd unknowingly avenged his death warmed my soul.

Chapter Twenty-Five

MALIAH

I'd been given a whole entire extra day and a half to get myself mentally prepared to tell Murk about Danny, but my nerves were still a fuckin' wreck.

"Mama, can you help the kids wash their hands? Dinner's almost ready," I called out while wringing my hands.

"How many times I gotta tell you, Maliah Michelle? These ain't my kids! They are *yours!*"

I felt myself begin to get heated until I heard the sound of her laughing from behind me. Whirling around, I looked into my mama's face and let out a deep breath.

"Of course, I'll help you out, baby," she told me. "I'm just playin' with you because you need to relax."

Watching her walk away, I took a deep breath and rubbed my hands against my thighs as I turned around to finish cooking. As much as I was less than thrilled about having her move in, I was grateful she was there because if Murk took the news about Danny the wrong way, I might need her help to get him off my ass.

"What you cookin'?"

Mid-stir, I froze in place when I heard Murk's voice behind me. I was so engrossed in my thoughts that I hadn't even heard him walk in. Taking a deep breath, I turned around and looked into his eyes, trying to gauge his mood. But of course, the blank expression on his face mixed with his piercing stare was like a wall. I couldn't figure out his mood at all.

"Just some food mama requested that I make. Peas and rice, chicken and—"

"Okay, so when in the middle of all this meal planning and shit were you gonna tell me you been chillin' with your dead baby daddy?"

My mouth dropped open as I tried to work my mind through how Murk went from meal prep to Danny in the same damn sentence.

"What are you talkin' about, Murk?" I asked him. My eyes darted towards where my mama had walked away with the kids to wash their hands.

"The fuck you lookin' over there for? Ain't nobody able to save your ass," he threatened in a low tone. "Answer my fuckin' question!"

I tried to move my mouth to say something but my jaw felt cemented in place.

"I—I—"

Just then, my mama walked in with the girls at her side and DeJarion in her hands. I felt a tiny sense of relief as soon as I saw them, but the heat coming from Murk's eyes told me that it was in vain.

"Okay, kids. You're all washed up so sit down so mommy can make your plates and—"

"MALIAH, STOP FUCKIN' AROUND AND ANSWER MY GOTDAMN QUESTION!" Murk yelled, scaring everyone in the room. "OPEN YOUR DAMN MOUTH AND TELL ME DID YOU FUCK THAT NIGGA!"

"On second thought, kids, let's go back down the hallway! BACK down the hallway. Let's go!" my mama ordered, snatching both the girls' hands in one of hers and rushing out the room.

"I didn't know he was alive!" I started from the beginning, trying my best to remember the lines I'd rehearsed. "Neesy told me he'd called her and said he was in the hospital getting surgery and—"

"Get to the point where this nigga ended up puttin' hickies on your fuckin' neck and layin' up with yo' ass at your mama house!"

"HUMPH!" my mama grunted as she walked in right after he said that and sat down at the kitchen table across from where we stood.

Crossing her arms in front of her chest, she planted her eyes right on us. Murk glanced briefly in her direction and she lifted her hand up.

"Don't mind me, darling, you can continue gettin' in her ass. I'm just here to make sure you don't *touch* her," she explained. "Other than that, we good."

After giving her a curt nod, Murk's attention traveled back to my face.

"Speak," he commanded in a flat tone that immediately made a shiver travel down my spine and all the way down to my toes. It was like the calm before the storm.

"He showed up after I finished my set at the club…"

My mouth went dry as I started to realize how fuckin' stupid what I was about to say would sound.

"I got scared because I saw some cars pull up and I thought you and your brothers were coming, so I left. I went to my mama's house and had a few drinks. I was drunk when he showed up—"

"Tsk, tsk, tsk…" my mama inserted her disapproval.

Tears began streaming down my face, and my vision became blurred so I was unable to see Murk's face.

"—I don't know what happened! I just know I woke up the next morning and he was in the bed. I texted Neesy and tried to get him out of there but then you showed up!"

"So you fucked that nigga then lied to me about it to my fuckin' face, Maliah?" he yelled as I dropped my head into my hands and began crying hysterically.

I heard sudden movement and the next thing I knew, Murk had grabbed me by both of my upper arms and was squeezing tight, but not enough to really hurt me. My eyes were stretched wide as I looked into his and, for the first time since I'd met him, I saw an emotion that caught me off-guard. He was hurt. The emotion was so raw and showed so deep in his eyes that my own began to tear up again just from seeing how badly he was affected by my stupid decision.

"I did but…" I couldn't even finish my sentence. "We have kids, Murk! You don't understand that. It's hard to just leave a man you got kids with!"

"FUCK THAT SHIT, MALIAH!" he roared. Then he narrowed his eyes. "I take care of you and them kids! Now you wanna tell me you owe your allegiance to that nigga because he gave you some kids he don't take care of! Maybe I should stop letting you swallow mine so I can get some fuckin' respect, huh?"

"WELL, GOTDAMN!" my mama commentated from her corner. I instantly regretted having her ass in the house.

Suddenly, I saw something shift in his eyes and the anger set in. It was almost like he became a different person. His grip became tighter and I winced in pain but tried not to cry out. He continued to squeeze harder and harder until I started to try and pull out of his reach.

"Murk—" I began.

"Hey, hey, HEY!" my mama called out but Murk's eyes were still filled with rage; it was like he couldn't hear a thing.

"Murk, stop!" I yelled out. "You're hurting me!"

I imagined that this must have been how it was when he killed someone. He blanked out and became someone else; someone heartless, disconnected and unfeeling. Someone totally void of all emotion.

"HEY!" my mama yelled out once more, picking up a frying pan and banging it hard against the counter. "GET YOUR HANDS OFF MY CHILD!"

There was another shift in his eyes and, all of a sudden, his expression softened. The hurt in his eyes returned and he released his grasp on my arms. Biting my lip, I rubbed my arm and looked at him as I backed further away from where he stood. The dark side in him had surfaced in a way that I'd heard of but never seen before, and I wanted no parts of *that* shit ever again.

"Do you realize how much I loved you, Maliah?" Murk spoke finally. "Do you realize that all this shit I've been doing for you…for the kids…I don't do this shit for no every day bitch! I'm not that kinda nigga! You always so caught up in what I say and how I say shit that you don't give a fuck about what I do—"

"That's not true, I—"

"IT IS TRUE! And don't fuckin' interrupt me when I'm talkin'! I'm the nigga around here taking care of your ass and you give all that up for a muthafucka that…"

He stopped and then balled up his fists at his side. "I should've made sure I'd killed that nigga when I had the chance."

"What?" I asked wondering if he meant what I thought by his statement.

Clamping his mouth shut, he stopped short and shook his head. His shoulders slumped down in defeat. Seeing him in a vulnerable state where he was wearing his feelings on his sleeve, threw me. For someone who seemed void of any emotion outside of anger or his normal careless nature, he was finally showing a side of him that I'd never seen.

"You won," he said finally. My eyes still damp from tears, I frowned at him, wondering what he meant.

"You won," he said again. "You can keep all this shit I've given you and still be with that lame ass nigga you really want. I'm out."

My heart skipped a beat as I watched him take the key to the house off of his keychain and lay it on the counter. He started walking to the door slowly, almost like he was dragging his feet and then opened it and left.

Seconds later after he'd gone, I was still standing, frozen in place, trying to deal with all of the thoughts merging in my mind.

"Damn, Maliah Michelle. Looks to me like you did the one thing that no one probably thought could ever be done," my mama said from behind me.

Confused, I turned around and looked into her face and waited for her to explain further.

"Baby…you broke him."

Chapter Twenty-Six

SHANECIA

"Listen, nigga, I ain't playin'! I been makin' progress with this shit!" Dame said as I rolled my eyes and sat at the dining room table with my book in my hand.

I was trying to pretend like I wasn't listening to him talking to Legend, but I was and I was getting a kick out of the whole conversation.

"Progress? Dame, it ain't even been that damn long!" Legend laughed at him.

"Muthafucka, what you *mean*?!" Dame asked with his hand to his chest like he was offended. "My baby ain't been here for over two weeks and I ain't shared her dick with none of these broads! Legend, give me some muthafuckin' credit!"

Legend laughed even harder and took a puff of his blunt as Dame narrowed his eyes at him.

"Nigga, I ain't giving you shit. You ain't *done* shit!" he told him. "The only reason you gettin' it together right now is because Trell left you and you want her back. The moment she comes back, your ass will be back hittin' up the hoes like normal."

Dame gave Legend a hard look and then his face suddenly broke as a dastardly frown crossed his face.

"S-S-So this mean you not gonna call her for me?"

"Hell naw, I ain't callin' her for you!" Legend told him. "Just relax and let things go. If it's meant to be, it'll be."

Legend reached out to hand Dame the blunt but he frowned and swatted it away. Shrugging, Legend placed it back between his lips and continued to puff on it as he relaxed in his chair. Smiling, I shook my head at both of them.

"So when we gonna move on this shit concerning Mello?" Dame asked quietly.

I could feel Legend's eyes move in my direction but my head was bowed and I was doing the best acting in the world to make it seem like I was fully engrossed in my book. I must have satisfied him because he sat up and leaned in towards Dame so that he could respond.

"I wanna move on it now but there is a hiccup in the plan," he told Dame. I could hear the annoyance in his voice.

"What's the hiccup?"

"I ain't heard back from Murk in two days. You know we ain't doin' shit without him. It's pissin' me off because he knows I need his ass on this. You spoke to that nigga?" Legend asked.

Totally engrossed in their conversation, I peeked over my book and saw Dame shake his head. Legend wasn't positioned so that he could see me so I continued to watch.

"Naw, I ain't heard from him but my phone been on silent the past few days. I been dodging texts and shit so I don't feel tempted to go run up in nothin'. This shit hard as hell, Legend. I been doin' all I can and you still don't wanna give a nigga no props! I been—"

"Dame, stop talkin' 'bout yo' dick all the muthafuckin' time! That's all you worried about and that's why you can't keep the shit in ya fuckin' pants!" Legend cursed. He looked over to me and I ducked my head down. Grabbing my headphones from around my neck, I placed them in my ears and started bopping my head to imaginary music.

"I ain't heard from Murk since he found out somethin' 'bout *ole girl*," he whispered so low I was just barely able to make it out. "I hope that nigga ain't done no stupid shit."

"Damn, I don't even wanna know what that nigga found out to make him disappear for two days," was Dame's response. "You asked Quan?"

Legend nodded his head.

"He ain't heard from him either? Damn."

Just then, there was a hard knock at the door. Dropping my book on the table, I jumped up to answer it.

"Neesy, sit yo' big head ass down!" Legend snapped just as I got to my feet. "I got that shit."

I rolled my eyes at Legend. "So it ain't safe for me to answer the door now?"

"No, it ain't safe for your gullible ass to answer the damn door. Don't think I forgot how that bitch played your ass at the warehouse," he added as he disappeared around the corner. "You still on punishment for that shit!"

Looking over to Dame, I placed my hand on my hip. "I don't know how you put up with his ass. I can't stand him."

Dame started to chuckle. "I don't have a choice in the matter, but you do, and you still stick around to deal with that hatin' ass nigga."

A frown crossed Dame's face for a second before he turned to me.

"Aye, you think I been makin' progress, don't you?"

The way that Dame looked at me as with pleading eyes changed my mood in an instance. Although Legend was slow to give him any credit, I had to admit that he seemed to really be trying to get things together for Trell. I hoped it would last. Sitting back down, I started to answer his question but before I could, I heard Legend's voice.

"Cush, what the hell you doin' here?"

"Cush?" Dame repeated with a frown.

He stood up and both of our eyes went towards the entrance of the house. Seconds later, a beautiful woman walked in like she owned the place. She was about 5'5 with long, dreadlocks dyed blond that fell at her waist. She was shapely to the point that I almost wondered if her body was 100% natural. With her large breasts, small waist and nice, rounded ass with thick thighs, I wasn't positive but, either way she had it going on. She was about a shade darker than Legend, with almond eyes almost the same color as her skin. Her style was on point and I assumed her brothers kept her incredibly spoiled because nothing on her looked like it cost less than a grand. She was the type of sister that Tanecia probably wished for when she looked at me.

As soon as my eyes fell on Cush, I could see the striking resemblance between her and Legend. If someone told me they were twins, I would have believed it. She looked like the female version of him and based on the way she walked in with her head held high in the air like she was the queen of the world, it was obvious she had his personality as well.

"Dame, tell your brother I don't need no invitation. I go where I want to go and he can't tell me what to do!" she said while rolling her eyes and gave Dame a hug.

Then her head rotated around to where I sat looking at her, and she shot me a small smile that didn't quite reach her eyes.

"You must be Neesy," she confirmed for herself in a condescending tone as her eyes raked my body, making me feel subconscious about my disheveled appearance. But, hell, I was lounging around my house! Wasn't no need for me to covered head-to-toe in designer clothing!

Although I wouldn't be dressed like that anyways, I reminded myself.

"Yes, I'm Neesy."

Standing up, I walked to where she stood with her hands on her hips and awkwardly held out my hand. With the edges of her lips curled up, she looked at it with disgust before begrudgingly reaching out with two fingers to shake it. Before she could touch me, I snatched my hand right back.

"You good," I told her with a frown.

She was standing in my muthafuckin' house! No way in hell this bitch was gonna act like that with me...Legend's sister or not.

Stunned by my actions, she froze, but then a second later an amused expression crossed her face and she smirked, reminding me instantly of Legend's signature smile.

"I *like* you!" she said all of a sudden, catching me totally off-guard. Then she turned to Legend. "Legend, where you find this chick right here? This my kinda bitch! Girl, give me a hug!"

Before I could respond, she turned around and pulled me into a tight hug while rocking from side-to-side as if we were old friends.

This heffa is crazy! I thought to myself.

I looked at Legend and Dame and noticed that both of them had bewildered expressions on their face. Scratching his head, Legend looked at Dame and he shrugged. When she pulled away, she rubbed her stomach.

"I'm hungry as hell. I know y'all got something to eat up in this bit—"

"CUSH!" Legend yelled out all of a sudden. "Sit your ass down and tell us why the fuck you here!"

"Yeah, sis," Dame chimed in standing next to Legend with his arms crossed in front of his chest. "You know you ain't supposed to be here. Especially ain't supposed to pop up without tellin' us. It ain't safe out here."

Rolling her eyes, she sat down at the table across from me and crossed her legs, as she gave a weary look to her brothers.

"Dame, tell me you not on that 'it's not safe' shit that Legend be on. I can take of my damn self! I'm a grown woman! You ain't my damn daddy, Legend!"

Frowning, she pointed right at Legend's face and I couldn't help but smile as I watched them. This entire argument was one I had with Legend on a daily basis. It's funny as hell how men tend to fall for women just like the women related to them. Cush had a mouth on her and she wasn't afraid to use it on anyone around.

"Yeah, you a grown woman! A grown woman that I muthafuckin' take care of!" he spat back. Cush shut her mouth but her eyes continued to shoot dangers at his face. Legend shot them right back, and a vicious staring contest ensued until Cush finally sighed and reached into her purse.

"Well, the reason I'm here seemed kinda silly to me after a while, but I was already on the plane so I had no choice," she explained, pulling out a letter. "I came home and I felt like someone was watching me. Then, in the middle of the night, I heard a noise and my window was wide open. It scared the fuck out of me so I packed my shit and hopped on the next plane. And while on the plane, I found this."

Reaching in her bag, she pulled out a piece of paper and held it out. Not stalling for a second, Legend walked over and snatched it away. Holding it up, he looked it over quickly as Dame peered over his shoulder.

"What da fuck?!" he cursed before scrutinizing the paper once more.

"That's what I said," Cush replied.

"I didn't even know this nigga was locked up…or alive. It says on here he murdered a whole damn family…kids and all. *And* tortured them," Dame said. "This some sick shit, yo. We do some fucked up shit but we ain't never touch no kids."

"And never fuckin' will. No matter what shit comes out my mouth when it comes down to it, I can't touch or hurt no kids…this nigga just as fucked up as I knew he was. If Quan hadn't stopped me, he would be dead," Legend gritted, balling up the paper in his hand.

Confused, I looked back and forth between all of them, waiting for someone to fill me in.

"Who?" I finally asked when I saw that it seemed as if none of them knew I was even sitting there.

"Quentin," Legend told me, the look in his eyes telling me that his brother being around was the last thing he wanted to hear. "So he been locked up all this time and now he's out. Damn."

"I think he's the one who's been watching me. I think he was in my house," Cush continued.

Both Legend and Dame narrowed their eyes at her and both walked in closer to her.

"Cush, you serious?" Dame asked and she looked at him like she wanted to slap him for asking. She was so much like Legend, it was insane.

"Of course I'm serious! You know what he did to me when I was little, Dame! I wouldn't joke about no shit like that!" she shouted.

Tears came to her eyes and she blinked them away as quickly as they'd come. I had no words at all and I definitely didn't want to imagine what her own brother might have done to her. This family had so many secrets and so many demons that I was starting to feel in over my head.

"Cush, you know if you would have told me about that shit right when it happened, I would have ended that nigga on the spot," Legend told her.

Dame shook his head angrily and looked away. Seeing Cush upset seemed to bother him more than he could deal with.

"I know but I couldn't…"

Swallowing hard, she shook away those words and then went back to the subject at hand.

"I wouldn't have thought it was Quentin except that a few weeks back, I thought I saw him but I wasn't sure. Legend, I called you to tell you about it but since you were on a trip with your boo-thang, you ain't wanna listen," she informed us, flicking her head pointedly in my direction. "I wasn't positive and I thought I was bugging, so I ignored it until what happened last night," she finished.

"Well, you're here now so you're good," Legend told her. He reached out and touched her hand to calm her down. I had to do a double take. Never before had I seen him act that way with anyone except for the few times he let his guard down around me.

"Where are your things? You can sleep in one of the rooms here," he told her. "You and Neesy can go shopping for whatever girly shit you need later on."

She nodded her head and glanced in my direction. I tried to smile but I couldn't move my lips. My mind was still settling on everything that I was hearing between the three of them. Legend and I needed to have a long talk. If he was going to have me involved in his bullshit, he needed to at least tell me enough so I wasn't walking around with my eyes closed.

"We gotta talk," I told him as soon as Dame had left to help Cush get set up in one of the rooms.

Pausing, he moved his eyes to me and I could see that his mood was nowhere near ready to deal with me or any of my questions. Hearing about his brother seemed to be affecting him even more negatively than when Mello's name was brought up.

"We will," he replied to me through his teeth. "Later."

And with that, he grabbed his phone, pecked at a few buttons and walked away. As I watched him leave, I reached in my pocket, grabbed one of the pills the doctor had given me and shoved it in my mouth. I swallowed it down dry and waited for its effect to kick in and carry me away.

My thoughts were starting to scream warnings in my head and I needed to silence them so I could have some peace. For the first time since I'd started falling for Legend, I was actually beginning to wonder if I could leave this life of crime, that I'd never even wanted, and go back to my boring ole life at Spelman.

Without him.

Chapter Twenty-Seven

MALIAH

It was funny how your life could go from sugar to shit in only a few minutes. Out of all the stupid shit I've done in my life, this had to be the dumbest. And it didn't help that almost every time my mama saw me, she would shake her head and remind me that she warned me. I wanted to strangle her ass. She loved to rub shit in when she was right.

The door swung open to my bedroom, the one I used to share with Murk, and I squeezed my eyes closed, pretending to be sleeping.

"Maliah Michelle, you ain't foolin' no damn body!" she yelled over my radio. Seconds later, the music came to a halt when she pressed the button to turn it off.

"Mama—" I started, sitting up.

"Girl, don't start with me right now! You in here looking sad as hell while you play Mary J. Blige on repeat. *First* of all, Mary J. ain't the one you need to be listenin' to, with your trifling ass! *You* cheated on *him*! He didn't cheat on you! Second of all—"

Placing my hand up, I tried to stop her before she got started.

"Ma, please. I really don't wanna hear all that right now," I told her.

She breathed out a long breath and her facial expression changed to one of sympathy, as she sat down in the chair across from my bed. Rolling my eyes, I fell back on the bed and stared at the ceiling. I was not in the mood for a lecture. For the last two days, the only reason I got out of bed was to care for my babies. Other than that, I'd been moping around the house, pissed off at myself for what I'd done.

"Have you heard from him?" she asked finally.

Tears came to my eyes and I shook my head. Although I'd been calling Murk back to back and sending him texts, he hadn't returned any of them. I was starting to think that I was blocked because the phone rang and rang when I called him, but the voicemail never picked up. I started to call Shanecia to ask her if she'd heard anything about him, but that meant I had to hear her lecture me about how stupid I was and I couldn't deal with that.

"I'm going to take the kids away for the day to give you some time alone," my mama told me. "But one thing I will say is that it's obvious he loves you. If he didn't, he would have kicked you out on your ass by now. He gave you everything and *he* left. Just give him some time, baby, and be smart. You may be able to save what you had."

Tears fell down my cheeks and I nodded my head. For the first time in a couple days, I felt hopeful.

A string of slob connected from my face to the pillow as I sat up to grab my phone that was ringing loud in my ear. Wiping it away, I sat up and grabbed it from the nightstand. It was a local number and, although I knew damn well it wasn't Murk, I answered it anyways.

"Hello?"

"Li-Li!" a voice said on the other end and I groaned. "I been callin' you!"

"And I ain't been answerin'! Danny, why the hell are you callin' me? Listen, we can't be together...we can go to court and figure out something with the kids later but just stop!"

"This got to do with that nigga, Murk, don't it?" he asked, his voice heavy with hurt. "I may been on that shit heavy back in the day but I ain't stupid. You with that nigga now?"

Sitting up, I clenched my teeth together before answering. I was getting mad as hell at Danny even though I knew I couldn't blame him for my decisions.

"I'm not with him anymore, thanks to you! He found out about us fuckin' and now we aren't together. Happy?"

There was silence on the other end for a second as Danny took in my words. Sighing, I got ready to hang up the phone. There was nothing else to be said.

"What you expect me to be, sad or some shit because you broke up with a nigga that beat my ass while we were together, and started fuckin' my bitch as soon as she thought I was dead? Get da fuck outta here! You wanted this dick and you gone always want this dick! That should teach yo' ass something—"

Angry as hell, I hung up the phone, cutting him short. Since blocking his cell didn't work, I made a mental note to just change my number. But then I changed my mind quickly once I realized that if I changed it, Murk wouldn't be able to call me if he wanted to.

I felt myself getting sad again so I picked up my phone so that I could look at some pictures that we'd taken together, thinking that it would make me feel better about everything. After about three minutes of looking at Murk and I when we were happy together, I couldn't take anymore. Pressing the button for my text messages, I decided to text Shanecia to see if she'd heard anything from him.

When I went to Shanecia's name, for some reason, I decided to scroll through our old messages and that's when I saw a video that I hadn't seen before. From the date on it, I'd sent it to her the night Danny and I was together.

"Oh God," I groaned to myself.

I didn't even need to click on it to know it was about to be some bullshit. Just from the preview I could see I was barely clothed and sitting inside my bedroom. Taking a deep breath, I mentally prepared myself to be embarrassed and pissed off as I pressed the play button.

"NEESY, you won't believe this shit!" I started in the video.

I was barely clothed, wearing only my top and nothing on the bottom from the looks of it…just like how I'd been when I woke up the next morning.

The video panned over to Danny who was knocked out, butt ass naked, in the bed with nothing but his tube socks on. Then I brought the camera back to my face. I was drunk as hell…my eyes were red and I was doing a terrible job at holding the camera steady. At one point, it was pointed straight up my nose while I spoke.

"This nigga came over here to talk, right? And being the bitch I am, I decided to shed some grace on a nigga and give him a taste of this pussy. Tell me why his ass ate my pussy, got ass naked so he could jack his dick and got mad because he couldn't get hard? Ole limp dick ass nigga almost cried his ass to sleep!"

Pulling away from the camera, I started laughing like I'd made the greatest joke in the world.

"That's right! *Limp dick*! This nigga done smoked so much of that *bullshit* he can't even get his dick to work when he want it! I'm so muthafuckin' pissed right now! Why the hell do I do this shit?"

Pursing my lips together, I shook my head as I watched tears come to my eyes in the video. Never in life had I seen myself this gone. I continued to watch while wondering if Danny's slick ass had slipped something in my drink.

"I just miss Murk," I confessed in the video. "Murk could always get it up. All that bitchin' I was doing about makin' love…I would be fine if that nigga would just come over and fuck me!"

Having seen enough, I turned off the damn video and threw my phone down. I couldn't take no more of that pitiful shit. Grabbing my phone, I started to delete it but then stopped suddenly. As embarrassing as it was, the video did prove one thing: *I did not fuck Danny.*

Sure, he gave me head but that wasn't as bad as what I'd thought happened.

Lying back on the bed, I started wondering how the hell I was going to use this newly acquired information to get back with Murk, when my phone rang. I grabbed it and prayed to God it was Danny so I could cuss his ass out for lying and making me believe we'd fucked when he called earlier. That nigga knew damn well he hadn't had none of this.

"Mali! I mean, Maliah…BITCH, where are you?!" a woman yelled at me through the other end of the phone. There was a lot of noise in the background so I guessed that probably was the reason she was screaming.

"Who the hell is this? And why the hell you yelling?"

"This is Candie. Now, where are you?!" she asked again.

Relaxing, I ran my hand through my hair as I answered her. "I'm home. You know I don't work there no more but…actually, I need to ask Tony for my job back 'cause—"

"Bitch, fuck this job! You need to get your ass over here *now*!"

"What? I—"

"Murk is here and his drunk ass just walked into a private room with Chyna's thirsty ass. From how she was dancing on him in V.I.P., I already know what her slimy ass is going in there to do! You need to get here quick and get your man because she already been tellin' these other hoes if she caught him alone, she was gonna fuck so—"

"Give me ten minutes. I'm coming to beat that bitch's ass."

Hanging up the phone, I got dressed in some sweats, a tank top and some sneakers. In less than three minutes, I was running out the door while pulling my hair up into a ponytail. I had a small container of Vaseline in my pocket and as soon as I started driving down the road, I pulled it out and began smearing it all over my face.

My nigga or not, Chyna was about to get fucked up for messing with Murk. It didn't matter if we were together at the moment, her ass was about to get it and I wouldn't stop hauling off on that hoe until somebody pulled me off her ass.

Boom! Boom! Boom!

"Bitch, bring yo' nasty muthafuckin' ass out here right now, ole tiger-striped ass bitch, I'm about to fuck yo' scary ass up! GET DA FUCK OUT HERE!" I screamed as I banged on the door to the private room that Candie told me Chyna and Murk were in.

"MALIAH!" Tony yelled from behind me. "You gone have to get your ass out my muthafuckin' club now! You scaring my customers!"

I placed my hands up to my temples and tried to calm myself down before I smacked the shit out of Tony. He must have felt it too, because he stepped back a few paces.

"Tony, if you don't let me tag this bitch, I promise on everything I love I'll be here every night waiting for her ass! So just walk away and let this happen because I promise you ain't gone be able to keep me away," I told him with sincerity.

Cutting his eyes to his bouncers, Tony crossed his arms in front of his chest and frowned, but he fell back. As far as he knew, I had the backing of the D-Boys because I messed with Murk, so he wasn't about to put his hands on me and none of the bouncers would either. He had no choice but to let me have my way.

As soon as they backed away, I went back to hauling off on the door as hard as I could. I couldn't wait until Chyna brought her raggedy ass out of the room because I was going to beat that bitch into the dirt and after I was done, Murk could get some, too, for trying me like this.

I heard the lock on the door click and I stepped back with my jaw clenched and my fists at my side. As soon as I got a glimpse of that bitch, I was going to knock the shit out of her ass.

The door swung open and the first person I saw was Murk. Candie was right. He was drunk as hell which was crazy to me. I'd never seen him that way before. Murk smoked blunts on the regular and, every now and then, he'd sip on some lean, but alcohol wasn't really his thing.

My heart fluttered when I saw his sexy ass but I was too heated for his presence to take my mind off what I'd come to do. Pushing him out the way, I stormed into the room looking for Chyna. When I walked in, there was no sign of her, but the side door leading to the private room on the other side was wide open. That bitch was trying to escape.

"MALI, I GOT HER!" Candie's voice rang out from behind her. "SHE TRIED TO RUN BUT I GOT THIS BITCH!"

Silently thanking Candie for being on my team, I ran out the private room and right towards where she was standing, holding Chyna down by her hair. Chyna's nasty ass was struggling and swinging as she tried to get away, but Candie was stronger than she was.

"Let that bitch go!" I ordered Candie and she immediately released Chyna's hair.

Chyna's neck snapped up once she was released and I threw a punch right at her nose.

Bam!

"Ah shit! Shawty got hands!" a man yelled from beside us.

Blood spurted out of Chyna's nose and she screamed. She tried to raise her hands up to shield her face, but I was on her like a fly on shit and I wasn't letting up. I started delivering punch after punch on her ass until she fell to the ground, covered in blood. She hadn't even been able to get fully dressed before she'd tried to run her nasty ass out of the room and, as she lay there naked, all I could think about was her fuckin' my man.

"Nasty bitch!" I yelled out as I continued my assault. But then my head reared back as I felt someone grab onto my ponytail.

"Get the fuck off her!" another bitch yelled. I recognized the voice as Trixie, one of Chyna's allies at the club.

Holding the sides of my head, I screamed out as Trixie drug me backwards by my hair, nearly pulling my hair from my scalp. And that's when two loud shots rang out, silencing everyone.

Pow! Pow!

Trixie let go of my hair and I fell on my back as she dove to the ground. People began to run and others followed her and dove down low to take cover.

"You know better than that shit," Murk's cool voice thundered through the club. "Keep yo' fuckin' hands off her."

Rolling around, I turned towards his voice and saw Murk with his arm lifted and his gun pointed in the air. His eyes were murderous and red with fury as he glared at Trixie who was cowering under his stare. I started to laugh and she cut her eyes at me like she wanted to try something.

"You wanna die tonight, bitch?!" he asked her as he lowered the gun and pointed it in her direction.

Coming to her senses, Trixie began to tremble with fear as she shrunk even further into the ground and away from where he stood.

"N—N—Noooo!" she cried out as tears began to fall from her eyes. "Please, don't kill me!"

Murk glared at her a minute longer before turning his glower onto me. His penetrating stare shook me to the bone and all sound faded away around me as I waited for him to speak.

"Get da fuck up!" he commanded.

Looking around quickly, I saw that all fearful eyes were on me as people pled silently for me to do whatever he asked so he could take his ass up out of there and they could leave with their lives.

Taking a deep breath, I stood to my feet and moved my eyes back to him. Without saying anything, he tucked his gun back in the waist of his jeans and pointed to the door. His hazel eyes that had been so cloudy and red just a few minutes earlier when he'd walked out the private room, seemed to now be clear.

I walked towards the exit of the club with my head bowed slightly. As I passed by Chyna who was trying to pull herself off the ground, I kneed her in the back and made her fall back down.

"You better not let me catch you again, bitch," I grumbled under my breath at her.

"Maliah, move your ass out the muthafuckin' club and shut that shit up!" Murk ordered from behind me.

Tossing her one last sneer, I walked out of the club with my head held high, happy as hell that I'd gotten a chance to beat Chyna's ass bloody. The way that Murk had bossed up on Trixie made me feel some type of way, too, the more I thought about it.

As soon as her ass touched me, he came up ready to bust on that bitch. No matter what went down between us, he was still my man.

"Why the hell would you do that to me?!" I yelled at Murk as soon as we were outside.

A few people stood around casting curious stares in our direction, but as soon as they saw I was talking to Murk, they decided they had somewhere else to be. Frowning, Murk scoffed at me as I looked him right into his face with my hands on my hips.

"Da fuck you talking about, Maliah?! You forgot why the fuck we ain't together now?"

"Yeah but—"

"Let me tell you this right quick," he said, cutting me off. "I was drunk, I fucked her and I remember every single part of it too." A malicious smile crossed his face when he said the last part. "She worked my dick good as fuck. Did all kinds of freaky shit that I didn't have to ask her to do. You wanna hear about it?"

Biting my lip, I shook my head and tried to blink away my tears. I knew what he was doing. He was hurting and he wanted to hurt me too. He was doing a damn good job at it.

"As far as I'm concerned, we're even. You good with that?" he asked me.

I couldn't even look him in his eyes from how much my heart was hurting. If he'd wanted me to feel as bad as he did a few days before, he'd done it. Nodding my head, I used the back of my hand to wipe the tears from my eyes.

Murk stood and stared at me for a few minutes and started to walk away slowly.

"Okay, let's go home then," he said.

Silently, I walked behind him feeling all kinds of emotions that I couldn't explain. Part of me was happy to have my man back, but the other part of me regretted even driving my ass down to the club.

But the biggest part of me…the part that I knew I should trust… knew that nothing would ever be the same.

Chapter Twenty-Eight

SHANECIA

"I wish you could see her, Tan," I told her as I sat beside her bed. "She's...she's like *you* but with my personality mixed with a lot of Legend's. It's crazy really. Honestly, I don't know how long I'mma be able to deal with her ass."

Tanecia laughed. She was beginning to look more and more like herself every day. I'd braided her hair back into a nice style after she complained about not being able to go get her hair done. Her skin was returning to its normal color and she was eating more so her weight was coming back.

"That ain't shit," Tanecia said. "If you've been able to put up with my ass for all this time, I know you can deal with her."

I nodded my head, knowing damn well she was right.

"Neesy, I know I've done some stupid shit...especially this most recent bullshit I've been involved in, but I've learned my lesson, I swear."

"Tan, we've all done dumb things," I told her, thinking about how I'd almost gotten myself and Legend killed the other day at the warehouse. "The thing is that we just have to learn from them. And you gotta know that you can't be lettin' a nigga treat you all kinds of ways and get away with callin' it love. You and Maliah both do that silly shit."

Tanecia turned up her nose. "Um…no, she was with a crackhead. That ain't the same thing."

"Okay, Danny was a crackhead and Mello was cracking your ass *upside* your head. What the hell is the damn difference?" I asked her while rolling my eyes.

Her lips poked out in a pout at my words, but there wasn't a damn thing she could say about it because she knew I was right.

"Listen, Tan…I gotta go check on my status at the new school I'm going to, so I need to get out of here before Legend calls to see where I am," I told her. She gave me a funny look and I caught it before she was able to neutralize her expression.

"What is it?" I asked her.

She pushed her lips together like she was about to say something but then changed her mind.

"Don't try it, Tan!" I pushed her lightly on her arm but she snatched back like I'd hurt her.

"Fine! Damn!" she yelled as she held her arm. "I was just going to say that after I got shot…okay, now this gonna sound weird as hell and I don't want you thinking I want your nigga because I don't, okay?"

On edge, I nodded my head and waited for her to continue. She swallowed and then started back talking.

"Okay…after I got shot, I was lying in the bed waiting for death to come because I just knew that bitch had killed my ass!" She punched her fist into the palm of her hand as she spoke. "Anyways, I was almost there…like I could feel it. I was cold and I know I was about to die because I started having visions of Grandma…"

Tears came to her eyes as she spoke and she shook them away. I felt myself start to get emotional as I listened to her and then out of nowhere, I heard Legend's voice in my head calling me a "crybaby ass girl."

"…I knew I was about to die but then the craziest thing happened.

I was staring up and I saw Legend's face above me…he was saying something to me like he was telling me not to go." She shrugged. "That's the last thing I remember seeing before I woke up here."

Blinking a few times, I stared at her incredulously.

"So let me get this right," I began. "You telling me you was about to die and out of all the niggas in the world you could think of dreaming about, your ass dreamt of *my* nigga?" I asked her with my hand pressed to my chest.

Tanecia rolled her eyes to the ceiling and sighed. "Neesy, like I said, I don't want your man so—"

"Oh, I know you don't want my man! Don't make me take that catheter out and lock you in this bitch so you can sit all day in a pile of your own shit!" I joked as I nudged her.

Why she was thinking about Legend, I didn't know, but I knew that Tanecia would never try me like that. We had our issues but we'd never betrayed each other like that.

"Why you had to mention that, Neesy? I know Darin told you I'm weird about it. I feel like I always smell like shit or something," she mumbled with a sheepish look on her face that made me laugh.

"Tan, you'll be able to get up and everything in a couple days, but I promise you, you do not smell!"

Standing up, I grabbed my purse and leaned over to give her a kiss on the forehead. She gave me a pressed smile and I giggled. She was still feeling some type of way about my joke.

"When will your nurse be back?" I asked her.

"In a few hours…I don't need her around as much now," Tanecia told me. I gave her a soft look as she looked out the window. Something was still bothering her but I didn't even have to ask what it was. If I was in her position and had almost lost my life after losing a baby, I would be the same way. She still hadn't mentioned a word about the baby and I knew it was affecting her in a way that I couldn't even begin to understand.

"You going to be okay on your own?"

"Yeah," she nodded her head. "I could use the quiet for a little while."

Taking her cue, I turned around and walked out the room and then the front door, making sure to set the alarm and lock it behind me.

"We got everything for you to start, you just need to pay the tuition for the first class and you're good to go," the admissions officer said to me with a less than enthused look on her face. It was only the afternoon and she already looked like she'd had a long day and hated her job.

"Thank you," I told her cheerfully and handed her my debit card. "I appreciate your help."

"Mm hmm," she grumbled and plucked the card from my fingers. "I'll be right back."

Sighing, I turned around and looked at the long line of annoyed students behind me and shot them a small, apologetic smile for holding them up. It reminded me of the day that I'd saw Legend at the gas station and he paid for my gas. A genuine smile crossed my face when I thought about that day. We were feeling each other way back then but were too stubborn to admit it.

Suddenly, something caught my eye and I looked up just in time to see a figure staring at me in the distance. He had a hat on his head, partially covering his face, but I still recognized him.

It was Quan.

Once he saw I'd spotted him, he ducked away and started walking away from me, dipping into the crowd.

"Quan!" I called out with a frown. He was acting strange. It wasn't like Legend hadn't asked people to follow me around in the past to make sure I was safe. Why would I be upset that he'd sent Quan?

"Here is your receipt. You're all finished," the woman said as she slapped the piece of paper down on the counter. "NEXT!"

I eyed her rude ass for a second before I grabbed my receipt, collected my things and left. My eyes swooped back down to where

Quan had been and I started after him to ask him to tell me what was going on.

Don't, was the single word that sounded off in my brain and I immediately stopped in my tracks.

If I'd learned anything the past few weeks, it was that I didn't need to question things that Legend did to protect me. He always had a reason and whatever it was, he'd tell me if he needed to. If he didn't, he always had a reason for that too.

Sighing, I walked to the parking lot and found my car. My mind was reeling with thoughts as I continued on. I began to get the creepy feeling that I was being watched, so I grabbed my purse firmer in my hand and started walking faster towards the car. Something wasn't right and the sooner I got home, the better.

Chapter Twenty-Nine

MALIAH

"I'm just tryin' to figure this out…so y'all together or y'all not?" my mama asked me as I was braiding Shadaej's hair.

"He hasn't said. He just told me that we were even and that was it. He hasn't really spoken to me since I saw him at the club so…I guess we not together," I told her.

I yanked a little too hard on Shadaej's hair and she let out a shrill howl. Sighing, I relaxed my grip and continued braiding.

"Y'all even? The hell do that mean? He like making you guess about where y'all stand, huh?" she inquired further.

"I guess so," I muttered.

Since leaving the club the night after I caught Murk with that bitch Chyna, we still hadn't spoken about where we stood as a couple. The crazy thing was that the past few days, he came over around the kids' bedtime to tell them goodnight and tuck them in, but he'd leave without saying more than two words to me.

It was fucked up how he was acting but I knew he needed his space. And he'd made it clear that he wasn't closing the door altogether so that left me with some hope. I'd finally told him that I hadn't had sex with Danny but it didn't seem to change much. He still ain't have shit to say to me.

My phone chimed and I grabbed it to look at the text message, hoping like hell it wasn't Danny trying to bother me.

Murk: I'm about to be over there.

Me: Okay.

Murk: Meet me in the garage in 5.

I frowned at the message before pecking out a reply.

Me: Okay…

Grabbing the part of Shadaej's hair that wasn't braided yet, I tied it up in a ponytail.

"We gone take a break…go ahead and play for a little bit," I told her. She was more than happy to get up and skip away from the pain of getting her hair done.

"Mama, I'mma be right back, okay?"

"Gone, girl, I'm reading my Bible," she said.

I squinted at the book that she had in her hand, noticing something odd about it. Standing up, I walked over to her and snatched the Bible, and another book that she had tucked inside of it fell out. The muthafuckin' Kama Sutra.

"Mama, what the hell you readin' this for?!" I yelled as I held the book out in my hands. Peeking at it, I saw a diagram of sexual positions that I never in all my life wanted to imagine her doing.

She stood up and snatched it out of my hand and grabbed her Bible with the other.

"That's *my* business! And you need to stay out of it!" She returned the book back to where she'd been hiding it inside of her Bible, and continued reading.

"What you need that for? Let me find out you got a man! I been noticing that you been going places a lot lately," I told her, but she kept her eyes on the book as if she couldn't hear me. "Then you got the audacity to wrap that up in the Bible like that! That right there might send you straight to hell!"

"Hell? Girl, everything in this book is natural," she retorted with a huff.

"Nasty ass..." I grumbled under my breath.

Shaking my head, I turned away from her and started walking down the long hall that led to the garage. My mama was on some other shit with her nasty ass. How the hell she was out in the open reading the Kama Sutra?

I continued walking and started thinking about how she seemed to be stepping out a lot for a few hours at a time. Since I'd stopped stripping, she'd even ducked out for a few hours late into the night and I'd catch her sneaking in.

Let me find out her ass been making booty calls! I thought to myself as I walked into the garage.

It was dark as hell inside, so I reached out to turn on the light but before I could, someone grabbed me by both of my arms, flipped me around to the wall and pinned me down. I opened my mouth to scream but when I felt Murk press his body up against mine, I closed my mouth shut.

Before I knew what was happening, Murk grabbed both of my wrists into his one hand and used his other to pull down my shorts off my hips. My breathing quickened and I felt myself getting wet as fuck. Reaching down in front of me, he pushed through my panties and stuck his fingers right into my treasure box. When he started moving back and forth in my honey pot while he rubbed his thumb across my clit, I moaned and turned to putty in his arms.

Then things got rough. Flipping me around, he snatched my shorts the rest of the way off and grabbed my shirt roughly in his hand, ripping it clear off my body. I couldn't see shit but, for some reason that added to the eroticism of it all. Our heavy breathing was the only sound, and hearing it made me even hornier, as I allowed him to take control of me. Grabbing the front of my bra, he pulled hard, almost burning my skin in the process until he'd ripped it right off. I was fully naked.

Peering into the dark, I waited for what was to come next. My eyes still hadn't adjusted so I couldn't even see an outline of him in front of me. The next thing I felt was his hot mouth wrapped around my nipple. I moaned in pleasure and then almost screamed out in pain when he used his teeth to bite down on it hard. He caught the scream before it could escape pass my lips, by enclosing my mouth with his, giving me a passionate but sloppy kiss.

"Open your fuckin' legs," he ordered but pushed them apart for me before I could even move.

As soon as they were open to his liking, he lifted me up, positioned me just right, and then slid me straight down, impaling me with his thick rod. I yelled out in painful ecstasy as he pushed his entire girth inside of me and started fucking the dog shit out of my ass, as he pinned me down on the wall.

"Oh God, Murk!" I cried out. "It feels so fuckin' gooooo—"

"Shut da fuck up!" he ordered, grabbing me around my neck and squeezing hard.

He kept squeezing until I thought he was going to cut off my breathing and I began to feel dizzy, but for some reason that shit had my pussy feeling good as hell.

"You think you gone fuckin' try me again?!" he roared in my ear.

"No," I wheezed out softly, which was all I could do with his hand wrapped around my neck.

"Louder!" he gritted as he continued to slam his dick into me so hard I thought he would bust down all four of my walls.

"NO!" I said a little louder.

"No, daddy," he coached me.

"No, da—"

"LOUDER!" he yelled as he bucked so hard into my pussy that I almost shot straight up the wall. My kitty was purring like a mutha-fucker for more, and I just knew I had to have dripped about a gallon of my thick, creamy honey all over his dick by this time. This nigga had my body going abso-fuckin-lutely insane!

"NO, DADDY!" I shouted.

"You gone fuck around with another nigga again?"

"No!"

"NO WHAT?!"

"NO, DADDY!"

Releasing my neck, he put both hands around my waist to give himself just the right grip that he needed in order to buck even harder.

"You gone give my pussy away to another nigga again?!" he shouted.

"NO DADDY!"

By this time, tears were streaming down my eyes. Never in my life had I cried during sex, but what this nigga was doing to me felt so damn good I just couldn't take the shit no more!

"What?!" he asked as he kept fucking the shit out of me.

"No daddy!"

"WHAT?!"

"NO DA—DA--GOTDAMMIT, I SAID FUCKIN' NO!" I screamed as I creamed all over him.

"Maliah, I love you," he told me just as my body began to tremble.

"Fuck! I love you too!"

The orgasm came before I knew it and I swear 'fore God that I saw rainbows and unicorns in that damn garage. The whole damn milky way came out of my pussy right then. Never in my life had anyone ever done that shit the way he'd done it. Fuck making love… if he wanted to do that to me for the rest of my damn life, I was perfectly fine with it.

He released me onto my feet and I crumbled the rest of the way down to the floor. There was no way in hell I was going to be able to stand after the assault he'd just laid on my pussy.

"Remember what the fuck you said," he whispered into the dark. "You try me again and I swear I'll kill your ass, Maliah. And no one on this fuckin' Earth will be able to stop me."

"Ye—ye—yes, daddy," I replied automatically, feeling drowsy as hell. All I wanted to do was lay down and go to sleep.

"Clean yaself up and get in the damn bed. Have my dinner ready when I get home. Daddy coming home tonight after work," he replied, laughing evilly at his own joke.

I heard some ruffling as he put his clothes on and got in the car. Standing up, I flicked on the lights just as he pressed the button to open the garage and turned on his car. I looked through the windshield as he backed away but his tint was so dark, I couldn't see shit.

However, I knew that he probably had that arrogant ass smile plastered across his face. He'd definitely come in here and did the damn thing. I'd be dreaming about that dick for days.

I tiptoed back in the house and ducked off into the laundry room so I could throw on some clothes and toss the ones that Murk had destroyed. Then I tried to creep by my mama to my room, hoping that she wouldn't hear me walking through the room.

"Well, hello Maliah Michelle," she greeted me while still looking at her book.

Sighing, I stopped creeping and just walked on by, giving up all together since I'd been caught.

"I guess you and Murk back together, huh?" she asked with a smirk, as she swiveled around in her chair to look at me. My cheeks flushed with red and I froze in place, more shame than I'd ever been in all my life.

"You *heard* me?" I asked her, mortified. The garage was clear on the other side of the five-bedroom house. You couldn't even hear when someone pulled into it, so I just knew for sure that she wouldn't have been able to hear me.

"I sure did," she replied, cutting her eyes at me. "I had to turn the cartoons up high in the kids' rooms so they wouldn't think someone was out there murdering you."

Mashing my palm to my head, I turned around and started back walking to the room even faster, so I could jump in the shower and hopefully forget this whole damn conversation.

"You callin' him 'daddy' and all but I'm starting to think they call him Murk in the streets because he be murdering that coochie—"

"MAMA!" I gasped.

"Tuh! Girl, don't act like I don't know about that stuff! I ain't been saved all my life. And you see what I'm reading!" she shot back. "But one question...who is the nasty ass now?"

Chapter Thirty

LEGEND

People thought I was crazy when I said the feeling I got when I was getting ready to unleash my anger on some niggas was almost the same as when I was busting a nut.

They didn't get it, but I got an exhilarating rush of adrenaline whenever the time came, and that was the only way I could describe it. Shanecia had the best pussy I'd ever been in, but even she couldn't relax me the way that it did when I laid down the law on some cock-roach ass niggas.

Finally, Murk had come to his fuckin' senses and stopped moping about his chick so we could handle business. As much as I wanted to snap on his ass for being gone for three damn days without checking in on anybody, I couldn't really be all that mad. If Shanecia had done the shit Maliah had, I would be gone much longer than the three days he'd had, and her ass would be gone *forever*.

In my opinion, Murk was on some friendly shit letting that broad live after doing the shit that she had. I understood that they weren't together at the time, but that shit didn't mean anything to me. In my book, Shanecia was mine and she always would be. Even if she left me, until I stopped having feelings for her ass, she belonged to me.

"She in there," Quan said suddenly. "I saw her through the windows in the back. I got the back door open so we good to go. A nigga in there too."

My eyebrows shot up in the air.

"Mello?" I asked him.

"Not sure, I couldn't see his face so I can't say for sure, but it's definitely a big ass nigga," Quan replied.

Dame clicked his tongue and nodded his head. "Well, let me find out that we caught this nigga sleepin'. That's what's up."

"Murk, you ready?" I asked him as he sat on the passenger side of the car. He was quiet as normal, but I could see the wheels in his head turning as he stroked the gun on his lap absentmindedly.

"I'm more than ready," he replied back.

"A'ight, let's go," I ordered and we all jumped out.

We ran around to the back of the house, trying our hardest to not be seen by ducking down under the large trees that lined the large property. To be the grimy ass nigga Mello was, he had some pretty good taste. As I ran through to the back, I made a mental note to upgrade Shanecia out of the spot I had her in when she finally got her flip ass mouth together. If this was the type of shit he had his wife in, I'd be damned if my lady gets anything less. She just had to check her attitude first so I'd know she deserved it.

As soon as we got to the back door, I opened it and we all ran up inside. The house was big as hell so although Quan checked it out as much as he could, we couldn't be positive there was no one else inside besides the two people he'd seen. Walking in, I had to admit that the house was just as luxurious inside as it was outside.

There were family pictures all over the house but I didn't pay any attention to them, until I heard Murk mutter behind me.

"This muthafucka got jits and shit!" he said in a low tone.

My eyes focused on one of the photos in the family room we were walking through. I stopped and stared at it.

"How the *fuck* this muthafucka hide a whole family and shit?" I mumbled as I stared at it.

It was a picture of Murk, his white ass wife and three little mixed kids. I had to give it to him, he was dumb as hell, but he'd even surprised the hell out of me with this.

"This nigga got him a white girl? What hood they do that in?" Quan joked while chuckling to himself. "I mean, I done been with a white girl or two, but they been them white girls with black on the inside, na'mean? This nigga went and got him a Becky—"

"Shhh!" Dame shushed him while elbowing him in the side. "You hear that?"

All of us froze in place and listened intently to whatever it was Dame heard. A few seconds later, a smirk crossed my face when I heard the light moans of someone in the middle of getting their dick wet.

"They in there fuckin'?" Quan whispered what we all were thinking. "I can't believe this shit!"

"Aye, when it's my time to go, I hope I die deep in some pussy. That's some G shit right there," Dame added with his eyes upwards, obviously picturing his statement.

I took off towards the stairs with Murk right behind me. Quan and Dame took up the rear, all of us with our pieces out.

"Nigga, I hope that's Trell's pussy you're imagining dying in. If it's another bitch, you'll definitely die up in her pussy, but it will be because Trell killed your ass," Quan whispered.

I gave him a look and he piped down and put his game face on. This was the chance we'd been waiting for and we had to do this shit right.

"OHHHHHH GAWWWDDD," the woman started to scream louder as we approached the top of the staircase. "Just like that! SHIT, this is so FUCKIN' GOOOD!"

We heard the squishing of wet pussy rubbing up on a dick followed by some smacking sounds. I squeezed my banger even tighter in my hand. Turning to Murk, I saw my nigga was already cocking his weapon, as Mello's bitch continued hollerin'.

"MUTHAFUCKIN' SHIIIIIIT! THIS PUSSY SO GOTDAMN GOOD!" the man bellowed, stopping all four of us in our tracks.

"What the fuck?!" Murk, Quan and Dame all said at one time.

Running up, I kicked the door all the way opened with my banger lifted up in the air, and fired off two shots. The bitch screamed and almost ran up the wall. Her nigga jumped right off of her, his dick wagging in the air as he turned around with his hands up in the air. When he saw my face, his brown face went as pale as could be as all of the color nearly drained away.

"That's right, nigga. It's me…muthafuckin' Legend," I said with my gun pointed at him.

Clicking his tongue against his teeth in disdain, Murk pulled up alongside me with his pointed at him as well. Quan and Dame moved to the side and grabbed up the chick as she screamed and hollered in sheer terror.

"Shut da fuck up 'fore I two piece yo' ass, bitch," Quan told her.

His normal humorous attitude had faded away and gave way to the goon that lie inside. Dame grabbed her by her golden, blond hair and threw her up against the wall, where she sat completely naked and trembling with two guns pointed at her head.

"L—L—Legend, it's not what you think!"

Squinting my eyes, I walked in closer, pressing the barrel of my gun against his left cheek.

"What da fuck you mean, Alpha? How the hell it ain't what I think? You in here in Mello's house, fuckin' his bitch, and you the one been giving that nigga information on us. You just one disloyal nigga, huh?" I laughed, but it came out coarse like sandpaper.

Terrified, Alpha was trembling so badly that his large, fat belly was jiggling in the air. He knew he was about to meet his end. There was no doubt about that, he knew how I rolled. Still, he had to try. I would listen for a few seconds since I'd promised his little brother I'd let him speak.

"I promise, I ain't never give that nigga nothin' that was all that useful, Legend! Sinai was the *real* snitch. He was givin' Mello information that led to shit. The only reason I was fuckin' with that nigga was because of Becky—"

"Wait! So this bitch's name *really is Becky*?!" Quan piped up, laughing his ass off. "I couldn't have imagined this shit!"

"—Rebecca," Alpha clarified. "I met her and I didn't know she was Mello's wife when I did…we started messin' around and I got caught up one day! The only way to get out of that shit was to tell him that I was trying to help him get you!"

"Oh, so you was doin' all this in the name of love?" I questioned him.

He nodded his head quickly in reply and let out a dry laugh.

"That's all it was…I ain't helpin' that nigga for real! I mean, if it wasn't for me, he would have killed Neesy!"

I started to feel myself get heated and I knew I was about to go the fuck off, but I tried to hold back for a second longer.

"Neesy? What da fuck you mean, nigga?" Murk asked from beside me.

Looking back and forth between the two of us, Alpha ran his tongue over his lips before speaking.

"H—He had me with him that day he injected her…When we saw her pull up, he was gonna kill her right away! I'm the one who told him not to kill her because he could use her to get you!"

This nigga stupid as fuck!

"So that was all your bright idea," I replied. "Oh, I get it." I looked over at Murk who shrugged and nodded his head.

"Yeah, makes sense," he added, making Alpha visibly relax.

It was funny to me how Murk played with these niggas and gave them hope in their last moments.

"Who else in on this shit? Omega been helpin' you too?"

He shook his head, "No, Omega don't fuck with Mello. You know he not made for this street shit…all he know is ball and—"

Pow!

Brains splattered all over, hitting Mello's bitch right in her face as Alpha's head exploded into pieces. His body dropped straight down to the floor as if it were tied with weights. The chick started hollering loudly until Dame lifted his gun to whack her in the head. She stopped immediately and started whimpering quietly.

Shaking his head, Murk lifted his weapon, walked over and pulled the trigger of his automatic, unloading his gun into Alpha's chest and stomach. Alpha was filled with holes before he was through. When he finished, he looked up at me, and then at Dame and Quan, who had shocked looks on their faces.

"What?" Murk asked with a shrug. "I had to make sure so we don't have no more niggas coming back from the fuckin' dead."

With that, he turned around and walked out the door, leaving me shaking my head. I looked at Dame and Quan.

"Gag her, bound her and let's go. Murk's gonna pull the car up so we can get out this bitch."

"N—N—No, please don't hurt me! My kids will be back from school soon and...please!"

Dame grabbed her by her head and started wrapping up her mouth first so she could stop with the pleading and begging. Him and Quan tied her up as I watched. Glancing at my watch, I thought about Shanecia. I needed to call her to make sure she was good.

"Y'all get her out real quick and then the two of y'all come back in to help me search this shit so I can see what we can find," I told them.

They grabbed her up roughly and I looked at Quan, as he gritted his teeth and assisted Dame. Ever since I'd questioned his loyalty a while back, he had chilled out with the questions, but I'd also noticed some distance between us.

"Dame, you can handle that for a few?" He nodded his head. "Quan, lemme holla at you."

When Quan walked over, I could tell he was still feeling some type of way but he wasn't saying anything about it.

"Aye, we need to just put all that shit from the other day behind us, a'ight? We brothers...I know you're not Quentin. So don't be walkin' around in here thinkin' that's what I got on my mind because it's not," I told him sincerely.

A smile crossed his face and he nodded his head.

"I accept your bullshit apology, Legend. You act like it'll kill you to say you sorry sometimes," he joked, reaching out to give me a half-hug. I returned it and then pushed his ass away.

"I ain't sorry. I'm a Legend, muthafucka," I reminded him smartly.

"No, yo' ass is a Leith! Don't be throwing off on the name mama gave you!"

Punching him in the shoulder, I said, "Shut the fuck up and help me search this shit so we can go, Quantinarion."

"Aww, nigga, you lame for that shit!"

Less than an hour later, we'd searched the house and came up on a good bit of info before we had to leave. Although there was more to look through, from watching the house the couple days before, Quan knew that a black SUV pulled in through the gates every day around the same time.

We didn't know back then that the SUV was transporting Mello's kids, but we did now. I was tempted to grab them up too, but it wasn't part of our plan and we didn't have everything we needed to tie them up as well.

"You thinkin' 'bout goin' after the shorties too," Murk said, reading my mind.

I nodded my head. "Yeah, that would definitely have gotten Becky back there talkin'. But I can't go on that right now."

"Naw, no can do. I draw the line at kids, Legend," Murk replied, shocking the shit out of me. "I know you ain't gone hurt 'em but I can't tie up no jits, man."

"When you draw the line at anything, Murk?" Quan asked, just as surprised as I was.

"Since he got shorties of his own, he done got a crack in that cold ass heart of his," Dame commented with a smile on his face. "That's so sweet, nigga!"

"Shut the fuck up, Damion. I been had a heart!" Murk replied, folding his arms in front of his chest.

I didn't say anything, but it was good seeing my nigga in love. Listening to them made me think of Shanecia, so I called her and let the phone go to the Bluetooth in the car.

"Hello?"

"Hey baby, guess what I got on underneath my—"

"Neesy, shut yo' freaky ass up! You on speaker!" I cut her off but couldn't help but laughing. "I got these niggas in the car with me."

"Oh, well tell them I said 'hi!'," she replied with a giggle.

"HEYYY NEESSYYY!" they chorused in response.

"Where you at, lil' booty girl?"

She sucked her teeth and I knew she was rolling her eyes. "I hate when you call me that shit. I'm walking to the car. I'm just leaving from on campus. By the way, when you see Quan again, can you tell him to stop duckin' and dodgin' when he following me? I saw his ass out here."

"Huh?" Quan said with a frown on his face.

I looked at him through the rearview mirror, wondering what the hell Shanecia was talking about and why Quan was following her. Murk and Dame must have been thinking the same because they all turned to look at him as well.

"I ain't been following her!" Quan piped up.

"Yes, you were!" Shanecia shot back. "Out here at the school like ten minutes ago, I saw you…Wait, how you get to Legend so fast?"

My chest tightened as I experienced the closest thing to fear that I'd felt in a long time. Every sound around me melted away as I stopped driving right in the middle of the road and thought about what Shanecia was saying. When I turned to Murk, his facial expression mirrored mine.

"Neesy…what you mean you just saw Quan?" I asked as I heard her shut the door to the car.

"He was out here watching me like ten minutes ago! This my second time seeing him watching me. Legend, don't try to act like you didn't send him to look out for me!"

Swallowing hard, I closed my eyes and clenched my teeth together.

"Neesy, get in the fuckin' car and get home right now!" I yelled. I wasn't angry with her but I was stressed as fuck.

"Legend…what did I do? What's wrong?" she asked her voice full of concern. "Quan was—"

"NEESY! Listen to what the fuck I'm saying!" I gritted. "Get home and get in the fuckin' house. That's not Quan that's following you. That's Quentin!"

"Oh my God!" she yelled out.

"Call me when you get to the house! I'll meet you there!" I told her.

Her phone hung up and I stomped on the gas. If Quentin was following Shanecia, he had a reason and it wasn't good. After all this time away, this nigga finally showed his face again, but I knew him better than to think it was an accident that she'd managed to see him.

If Shanecia had spotted him, it was because he wanted to be found.

Chapter Thirty-One

MALIAH

"Maliah, wake up!"

My eyes shot open instantly and I gasped out loud. I'd been having a crazy ass dream and, for once in my life, I was happy about my mama nudging me awake. I sat up in the bed and frowned at the worried look on her face.

"What's wrong?" I asked her as she sat on the bed next to me.

"I'm telling you this just because you need to know and that's it. No other reason, okay?" she asked, giving me a pointed look.

Taking a deep breath, I nodded my head.

"Berneice called me…she said that Danny is back 'round where y'all used to live." She paused and my heart felt like it was twisting up in my chest. "He's back using again."

"What?!" I said. "He's using? But he was…I don't get it! He was just fine, how could he…"

My voice trailed off as I began to think on things. No matter how much I tried to tell myself that I was not to blame for Danny going back to drugs, I couldn't help but feel that way.

If I'd been there to help him, he wouldn't have done it…

"I know what you're thinkin' but it's not your fault," my mama told me. Her own eyes were damp as if she'd been crying.

"He made the choice to do what he's done…there is nothing anyone could have done about it. If that's what Danny wanted to do, that's what he was going to do! Even if you would have gotten with him…the first time you all faced difficulty, that's what he would have turned to in order to cope. You can't change that."

I nodded my head as I listened to her. She was right.

"I just want to check on him one last time…can you go with me? I need to do this but I don't want to do anything that will anger Murk so I need you to—"

Lifting her hand up, she stopped me mid-sentence. "You don't have to say another word. I was actually going to go check on Daniel myself. Let's drop the kids off with Berneice for a few minutes and then see if we can find him over there. I want to pray with him and then we can go."

Nodding my head, I sighed and got out of the bed. I threw on a hoodie over my tank-top and pushed on my sneakers before going in the room to get the kids together. Five minutes later, we were in the car and heading over to my old side of town.

Everything was just as I'd left it. The same niggas who were always sitting on the corner were still there. The same thirsty chicks who were always trying to get their attention were there, too. Everything had changed for me but nothing had changed for them. It was all the same.

After dropping off the kids, I turned to look at my mama and she nodded her head in encouragement.

"She said he was around here just walking around. I can't imagine where he's sleeping…since your old place is burned down, where else would he go?"

I didn't answer her because, at that moment, we were driving past my old place and I couldn't help but think back to what Murk had said when we were arguing that one day.

"I should've made sure I'd killed that nigga when I had the chance."

Shivering, I tried to wipe those words from my mind as we

continued to search the neighborhood. Fifteen minutes later, we'd circled the block a few times and still hadn't seen him. It was starting to get dark and I wanted to get back home since Murk had mentioned coming back for dinner.

"Should we ask some people if they saw him?" my mama inquired.

Shaking my head, I kept on driving. "No, these people know Murk and I don't want to risk anything getting back to him."

Just then, something caught my eye. It was Shanecia's mama's apartment and her front door was wide open.

"Aw, hell, her ass probably in there high with her damn door wide open," I grumbled under my breath as I pulled over to the side of the road.

"Who?" my mama asked.

I pointed to the apartment. "Alicia...Neesy has been trying to get in touch with her. Let me see if she's in there and at least shut her damn door."

Grunting, my mama crossed her arms in front of her and leaned back in her seat.

"Well, you can do this one *without* me. You know I can't stand her ass," she replied.

With a soft chuckle under my breath, I placed the car in park and got out. I didn't even have to walk into the house to smell the strong, pungent odor of spoiled food and whatever other nasty shit Alicia had up in there. It was crazy to me how far she'd fallen.

I shouldn't be too damn surprised, I thought as I walked inside and scrunched up my nose in disgust at the condition of the apartment. *Danny has fallen just as low as she has.*

Other than the trash that was littered all over, along with the plates of half-eaten food and open beer bottles, there was nothing and no one in the front room, so I continued to the back. Marching straight to Alicia's room I banged on the door a couple times.

"Alicia! Are you in there? It's Maliah!" I shouted although I knew if she was high, I could forget about her answering.

Sure enough, there was nothing coming from the other side so I reached down and tried the handle. It was unlocked.

When I opened the door, the sight in front of me almost made me lose my entire mind. My mouth fell open as I squinted in the dim lighting to make sure that I was definitely seeing what the hell I thought I saw.

"Oh my God!"

Placing my hands to my mouth, I took a step into the room and then froze in place as I looked down at the scene in front of me. Alicia was lying on the dirtiest mattress I'd ever seen in my life, butt-naked and unconscious. But the person lying beside her is what would have broken my heart if he hadn't already broken it a thousand times.

It was Danny. Like Alicia, he was also naked and unconscious. I leaned in close to make sure the two of them were breathing before I turned on my heels and walked the hell out of the house and to my car. I didn't even bother closing the front door. That's how much I didn't give a fuck.

"Was she good in there?" my mama asked as soon as I got into the car. She looked back at the front door. "Baby girl, you didn't close the door!"

"She's good," I said in a voice that was completely void of emotion.

Hitting the gas, I took off down the street to get my babies so I could get home and cook for my man before he got home. As soon as he was done eating, I was intent on running him a shower and fucking him in it and then out of it, however he wanted; anything he said goes.

After seeing what I'd just seen, there was officially nothing keeping me from giving my entire heart to Murk because I was so through with Danny that, in a few days, I was certain I would forget that nigga's last name. I just couldn't wait until I told Shanecia this shit.

SHANECIA

My breath caught up in my throat when I felt someone grab my phone out of my hands and hang up on Legend. Out of the corner of my eyes, I saw a flash of movement behind me and my eyes rotated to the rearview mirror where I instantly was able to put a face with the name.

"Quentin?" I said as I looked at him.

Without saying a word, he nodded his head.

Quentin looked exactly identical to Quan minus one thing: he had a long, jagged scar coming down the side of his face. His eyes were wild and untamed, almost crazy even. It gave him a look that made all the difference between him and his brother. Whereas Quan's eyes were light and humorous and inviting, Quentin's seemed to be harsh and full of evil intent.

"Drive," he said finally as he lifted a single finger up and pointed ahead of me.

Trying my hardest to remain calm, I swallowed hard and turned on the car.

"Where to?" I asked him as I pulled out onto the road.

I flinched when I felt him press the cold barrel of a gun against the back of my neck, and jumped again when I heard the click that followed.

One in the chamber, pull the trigger and shoot... I thought, repeating the words that Legend had told me when he was showing me how to use a gun.

"Drive to your home where you live with my brother," he ordered finally. "It's been a long time and I'm ready to see my family."

TO BE CONTINUED

Note from Porscha Sterling

Thank you for reading! I swear, I don't know what to really say about this group!

Legend & Murk are finally learning how to love. Imagine that! The rudest men in the world have developed a soft spot for a woman. In this part, you get to see WHYthey have those issues. The past can haunt us but only if we let it! Hopefully, the two of them can continue to be the men Shanecia and Maliah need and shed some of that thug of them…at least when it comes to their ladies.

Shanecia seems to be adjusting to her role as Legend's Street Queen, huh? The more that Legend tries to show her what it means in order to survive in the streets, the more she seems to rise to the occasion. But after another deadly run-in with one of Legend's long-lost enemies, will she survive? And if she does, will she tell Legend that's she's had enough? And what will he do once he realizes he's failed to protect her…once again?

Maliah means well but she's tortured by her bad luck! Do you think that she's had enough of Danny for real now? Do you think there is ANY excuse he can give her to make it better? And what will happen when she tells Neesy about her mama and Danny?!

Tanecia & Darin weren't in this sequel all that much but GUESS WHAT? They will definitely be in part 3 so get ready. And…YES, there will be a lot of drama! Will Darin be thug enough to keep her interest or will Tanecia let her attraction to dopeboys pull her away from the only man who has REALLY loved her?

Get ready because PART THREE IS COMING SOON!

Please make sure to leave a review! I love reading them!

I would love it if you reach out to me on Facebook, Instagram or Twitter!

Also, join my Facebook group! I love to interact with my readers. If you haven't already, text **PORSCHA** to **25827** to join my text list. Text **ROYALTY** to **42828** to join our email list and read excerpts and learn about giveaways.

Peace, love & blessings to everyone. I love allllll of you!

Porscha Sterling

Text **PORSCHA** to **25827** to keep up with Porscha's Latest Releases!

To find out more about her, visit

www.porschasterling.com

CPSIA information can be obtained
at www.ICGtesting.com
Printed in the USA
LVHW040015010319
609156LV00003B/211

9 781946 789037